THE *secrets* WE HELD

Secrets & Truths Duet
Book One

D1528304

New York Times Bestselling Author

e.k. blair

To Sally
for always believing in me and my visions

We are the voices for the voiceless, and we tell their stories.
We—because I couldn't do this without you.

THE secrets WE HELD

One

KATE

"Hey, Piper," I call out as I rummage through the huge mess of mail and junk that's been piling up on the kitchen counter for God knows how long. "Have you seen my new leash. I just bought it, and I can't find it anywhere."

"You getting kinky on me, Kate?" my best friend since high school says when she emerges from her room.

She saunters into the kitchen with a smirk on her lips, and I laugh and shake my head. "It's my new leg leash."

Her eyes widen at the same time her smile grows. "I always knew you had a hidden sick side."

"I'm serious." In my search, I grow frustrated. "This place is a disaster, I'm surprised we can find anything."

"It's not *that* messy."

A couple of magazines fall onto the floor as I continue to dig through the random piles that are spread all over the kitchen and living room. "Do you even read this shit?" I ask when I pick up a random cooking magazine. "You don't even cook."

"That doesn't mean I don't aspire to"—she snatches it out of my hand—"one day."

"I've known you since my sophomore year of high school and not once have I seen you cook."

Perching a hand on her hip, she says, "It wasn't my fault that my parents hired housekeepers and chefs to do the cooking. That doesn't mean I don't want to learn some day."

Growing up in West Palm Beach was a trip. On my side of the intracoastal, there's a certain level of affluence, but when you cross the short bridge over to Palm Beach, you're in a world of opulence. That was where Piper grew up.

We are different in many ways, but alike as well. She was over the snooty sense of entitlement at the private school and begged her parents to transfer her into a public school out of Palm Beach, which was when our paths crossed.

Aside from Piper, I don't have a lot of girlfriends. My main hobby is surfing; it always has been, which is why most of my friends are guys. It's easier that way—drama has a shorter life span with them than with girls who seem to feed on it like they need it for survival.

"Found it!" I grab the plastic bag and pull out the new leash for my surfboard before shoving it into my backpack with my wetsuit, zipping it up, and slinging it over my shoulders.

"Dinner tonight?" she asks.

I give her a hurried, "Sounds good," as I get my board and rush out of the condo we share.

When we decided to come to the University of Miami, it was a no-brainer that we'd be roommates. Aside from her messiness, she's an easy person to live with. Unfortunately, she doesn't have a cleaning staff to pick up after her like she did back home.

It's unfortunate for me too.

Miami traffic is a nightmare, and when I finally make it to the beach, the guys are already in the water.

After I pull on my wetsuit, I wax down my board, attach my new leash, and paddle out.

"Where you been? Waiting for your nails to dry?" Brody teases as I swim up to him.

"Don't even come at me with that." I sidle next to his board and sit up. "It's crowded out here today."

"Swells are amped," he says. "Come on."

I spend the next hour or so catching waves that break perfectly. After a while, I grow frustrated with having to fight for each wave with the number of people out here and decide to swim in for a breather.

After setting my board aside, I sit in the sand and take a gulp from my water bottle as I look out into the ocean. It's the end of October, which means most of the tourists have been swapped for the local surfer crowd. Travelers flock to the shore in the summer, but the waves are the best during this time of the year.

Brody catches a decent ride before he and a few other guys paddle toward the shore. When they hit the sand and start walking my way, I spot Micah and his long, bright blond hair. He's out here often with Brody, but it's the guy with shorter sandy blond hair who catches my eye.

"You got one of those for me?" Brody asks when he flops down by my side, and I toss him an extra bottle of water.

"What's up, Kate?" Micah greets as he sets his board aside and takes a seat in the sand.

I give an acknowledging nod but quickly turn my attention to his friend when he complains, "What's up with the fucking newbs out here today?"

He runs his hand through his wet hair, spiking it as he does and sending droplets of water off the ends to land on his broad shoulders.

"Kate, this is my buddy, Trent," Micah says, and I flick my eyes up to his friend's, hoping nobody saw that they were just on his chest.

"Hey."

I smile. "Hey," I offer in return, feeling like a total dimwit.

No one gives me a double glance, so I brush off the paranoid thought that, somehow, they can see the stupid butterflies that have me frazzled.

"We need to get out here at sunbreak. I have to get in some decent practice before next weekend," Micah says, and Brody agrees.

"Eight days and counting," Trent notes about the surf competition in Deerfield Beach.

"Exactly. There's not a lot of time left."

Brody crushes the bottle of water as he chugs the rest of it. "Let's not waste it, man."

The two of them get up, grab their boards, and head back out, leaving Trent and me alone. That damn tingling in my belly annoys me, mostly because I'm not the type of girl who gets stupid with guys, and yet, here I am, stupidly gazing at him.

"That yours?" He eyes my board.

"Yeah."

"It's clean." He then looks over at me. "I almost mistook you for a bunny."

My jaw drops slightly, and he grins.

"You offended?"

"That you assumed me to be a bunny? Yeah. Majorly offended."

When he hears the annoyance in my tone, his grin breaks into a full smile and he laughs under his breath. I despise bunnies—the girls who flock to the sand in hopes of getting noticed. They're trite and far from who I am. Or are they? Right now, I'm a little lost in his unique eyes, which are two different colors: hazel and blue. The blue isn't very vibrant, though, which makes the difference not so noticeable.

"How long have you been surfing?"

I break my stare and glance away just in time to see Micah

catch a killer wave. "Since I was old enough to ride a bike. My dad taught me."

"You from around here?"

"West Palm Beach," I tell him. "You?"

"Tampa."

"That sucks."

He shoots me a side stare and then agrees. "No shit. It's nice to finally have some decent waves."

I've never been to Tampa, but everyone knows the west coast of Florida blows for surfing. The water is hot and flat.

"Are you at the University of Miami too?"

He nods.

"What are you studying?"

He gives me a perplexed look, and I press, "Your major?"

"People declare that shit this early?"

I chuckle. "Um, yeah."

"Nah, man." He shakes his head at the idea. "I try not to plan the future."

"Isn't that the whole point of college?"

"Maybe for people like you."

"You say that like you know me."

Sitting to my side with his arms resting on his bent knees, he wears a cocky smirk. "Are you some sort of an enigma?"

I quirk a brow. "No."

"Then I pretty much know you."

In a snap, my gaze turns into a glare. "What's that supposed to mean?"

"You girls are all the same. You want to believe that you're different, but you're not."

"That's fucking sexist."

"It's the truth," he defends. "Humans are simple creatures, but for some reason, women think it's a bad thing to be simple,

5

so they purposely complicate everything because, in a weird way, it makes them feel special."

"You must be quite the charmer."

He winks, and I hate that it comes across as sexy when it should irritate me. "You know it!"

"What the fuck are you doing?" Micah shouts from the water. "You look like you need a carrot."

"Eat dick!" Trent hollers back at the insinuation that he looks like a bunny sitting in the sand.

Without another word, he grabs his board and jogs into the water. I'm unable to pull my eyes away from him as he lies on his board and digs his arms into the water. The fluttering returns, and I silently scold myself for staring like a schoolgirl. The beaches are crawling with charming and carefree guys just like him. I bet he also trolls the shore to pick up unsuspecting girls who are here on vacation. I'm sure he gets a kick out of being the summertime fling story they go home and tell their friends about.

I roll my eyes, feeling a tad jealous as I do.

What is wrong with me?

Two

KATE

"HEY, THANKS FOR LETTING ME TAG ALONG."

"Yeah, no problem," Brody responds as we make the drive to Deerfield Beach. He then reaches over and turns down the volume to the music. "So, any reason why you didn't register? It isn't like you aren't good enough."

"I love surfing, but it's really only a hobby. It's the one part of my life that holds zero stress for me. The last thing I want to do is suck the fun out of it by turning it into a job."

"I get that. But, still, it'd be a killer job."

"Is that what you want to do? Surf professionally?"

He exits the highway as we near the hotel. "Yeah. Micah and I were talking about it a couple of months back. Even if I never make it to the pro level, just to snag a sponsorship would be cool."

"I'd be down with taking a sponsorship. Being paid to wear someone's clothes or use their gear . . . sign me up."

"Not going to happen unless you get your ass registered in some of these comps."

Comps aren't my thing. I would never admit this to anyone, but the only reason I asked Brody to let me tag along is because Trent is going to be here.

God, I am so lame. I'm an embarrassment to myself.

I haven't seen him since we met at the beach last week. And because our paths haven't crossed on campus, I figured I could make them cross this weekend.

"Shit, this place is packed," Brody complains when he turns into the hotel parking lot.

I'm not sure why he's surprised. This competition is one of the largest qualifiers in Florida.

When he manages to find a parking spot, he unfastens his seatbelt and asks, "Would you mind grabbing my boards while I check in? I don't want to leave them out here, and I definitely don't want to drag them around with me in the lobby."

"No worries. I'll take my time. I need to call my dad anyway."

"Cool. I'll catch you inside."

He combs back his long brown hair with his hand, slips on his baseball hat, and hops out of the car, tossing me his keys through the open window.

I'm already on the phone when I respond with a simple, "Okay."

"Kate," my father answers enthusiastically. "How's the competition going?"

"We just got here. Brody is checking in, but I wanted to call you before this weekend got too busy."

"It's too bad you aren't competing."

"Dad . . ."

"You'd put the men's division to shame," he dotes before adding, "I remember the day I got you on the board."

I smile, and even though I can't actually recall the first time he put me on a board, I know the story by heart.

"You were a natural, giggling when you actually stood up and caught your first wave. Your mother was so excited, I could hear her cheering from the shore."

My father has always been one of my biggest cheerleaders, and there was a point in high school when I did want to take the sport to the next level, but that all changed a couple of years ago. It isn't something my dad likes to talk about because deep down the accident really scared him.

"You know, you could enter a competition just for fun. It doesn't have to be anything serious."

"I'll pass." I try to brush off the conversation, but he doesn't take the hint.

"You have a gift."

"What's Mom doing today?"

"Always quick to dodge conversations." He chuckles. "She's out shopping with your sister for a dress for the Sadie Hawkins dance."

Audrina is a sophomore in high school, and the girl is boy crazy, like *crazy*, crazy.

"Who did she ask?"

"Some kid she can't stop talking about. He plays lacrosse and is on student council."

"You're going to give him hell, right?"

"You know it!" He laughs.

"Dad, I have to run. Tell everyone that I miss them."

"I will. You have fun this weekend."

We say our *I love yous* before I shove my cell into my pocket, hop out of the car, and unstrap the boards from the roof.

After I meet back up with Brody and we dump everything off in the room we're sharing, we pick up his heat pack and head down to the water.

Another age division is already in progress, and we have a few hours to kill before Micah goes out.

"I see the guys on the other side of the media tent."

We head over to where our friends are hanging out and

discuss heat times. Eventually, Trent walks up with his arm around some blonde. There's a coiling in my stomach when I see them together.

"What's up?" he says, clapping hands with each of the guys.

"Who's this?" Brody asks of the girl.

"This is Ady."

Everyone introduces themselves to her before she takes a step away and they go back to talking about surfing. She appears uncomfortable. Even though I have no desire to talk to a bunny, I'm not a bitch.

"So, you're here with Trent?" I ask as I sidle up next to her.

She gives a nod.

"I didn't know he had a girlfriend."

"Oh." Her eyes widen and flick to mine. "No. I'm not his . . . we're not . . ."

My stomach uncoils in relief. "Sorry. I just assumed—"

"We're just friends, that's all. We went to high school together."

"Oh." I guess she isn't a bunny. "Do you go to UM, too?"

"I'm taking the semester off," she says, darting her eyes to Trent a time or two, which makes me wonder if she's crushing on him as badly as I am. Who could blame her? He's hot.

"Hey, what're you doing?" Micah calls out as he jogs over to where Ady and I are standing before turning his attention to me. "Kate. I didn't know you were coming."

"Yeah. So, when are you competing?"

"Later today. Did you enter?"

"No, I just came to watch."

"Sweet." He then turns to Ady. "I'm going to run up to the room and lie low for a while before my heat."

"I'll come with you," she tells him.

"You sure?"

She gives him a nod, and I figure it's Micah she's seeing instead of Trent.

"It was good meeting you, Kate," she says.

"You, too. I'll catch you later."

I watch them walk back up the beach hand in hand, confused as to why both guys are affectionate with her. Then I'm confused as to why I even care.

After a while, the group disperses and gets ready to hit the water. Since Trent and I are here as spectators, we find a spot to sit and watch. Despite the fact that I'm a super relaxed person, being with Trent when no one else is around makes me super uneasy, but I'm not about to show that, so I feign coolness.

"So, why aren't you out there?" I ask as the foghorn blows, signaling the end of the heat.

"Because I don't want to turn what I love into a chore."

I stifle a smile because I pretty much said the same thing to Brody earlier. Most want the sponsorships, the titles, the fame, and the money. Not me. Well, aside from a sponsorship. I'd take that any day.

"What about you?"

"Same reason."

He laughs under his breath, and I turn curious eyes to him.

"What's so funny?"

"Sure you're not scared of looking like a poser?"

I slug him in the arm.

"Dude!" he whines, rubbing the sore spot. "Treat your boy a little more delicately."

"Delicately?" I laugh. "And you are not my boy."

"That hurts worse than your beating."

"I'm sure."

As the next group of guys paddle out, I lean back on to my elbows in the warm sand. Even though it's overcast, the heat from the hidden sun radiates off my skin.

A faint tapping draws my attention, and when I glance over at Trent, he's clicking a vape pen to turn it on.

When he slips the pen between his lips, he catches me staring and lowers it. "Pardon my manners," he quips before holding it out to me. "Ladies first."

My eyes narrow.

"What?" he defends. "I don't need you accusing me of being sexist again."

"You're a shit, you know that?"

He nods. "Yep."

I grab the pen and take a pull. As I hand it back, I hold the fumes in my lungs long enough to feel the initial hint of the impending high.

"So," he says after he takes a hit, "you're a Palm Beach snob."

"*West* Palm Beach."

"As if that makes much of a difference."

"Tell me something . . . are you capable of having a normal conversation without being insulting?"

"Are you insulted because it's the truth?"

There's no controlling my rolling eyes. "You're annoying."

The corner of his lips lift.

"And obnoxious."

"Look at who's being insulting now." He takes another pull from his pen.

"Just calling it as I see it."

"Same here," he says as he blows out the remaining fumes. "That being said, you should come out to dinner with us later."

Trying not to expose my slight elation, I give him a glare. "You're inviting me out to dinner five seconds after calling me a snob?"

"No, I'm inviting the guys, which you happen to be a part of. Unless you'd rather it just be you and me." He wags his brows, and the foolish love-struck girl inside me is jumping up and down, but I stifle my excitement and fight back the smile that's tugging on my lips. No way do I want him to know just how eager I am to spend more time with him, even if that time includes everyone else.

"An evening alone with you throwing jabs at me? No thanks."

"For the record, you're the only one who's thrown a jab." The guy actually rubs his arm to emphasize his point, but I shake my head and go back to watching the surfers.

The next handful of hours pass as Trent and I watch the guys throw down their best in the water. Micah ranks impressively high, coming in fourth while Brody places a respectable twelfth. After taking a quick break to clean up, we do, in fact, join Trent and his friends for dinner. While the rest of us talk enthusiastically about the competition, Ady sits quietly, barely saying a word and hardly eating anything. After five minutes of watching her push food around her plate, I settle back in my chair.

"You not into all the surf talk?" I ask, not wanting her to feel left out.

She shrugs. "It's okay, I guess. Between Micah and Trent, I'm used to it."

"Have you known them long?"

"A couple of years. I met them when I moved to Tampa during my junior year."

"That must've sucked, having to change schools like that. Where did you move from?"

"Texas." She stabs a piece of broccoli with her fork. "What about you?"

"She's a Palm Beach snob," Trent responds, butting into our conversation.

"*West*," I correct pointedly before turning back to Ady. "*West* Palm Beach. Your friend doesn't seem to know the difference."

"Just ignore him," she tells me, and when I look over at him, he shoots me a wink.

"Is he always this charming?"

"Sometimes he can be a pest."

"You mean this is him *not* being a pest?"

"Don't throw me under the bus, girl," he playfully warns Ady, which causes her to laugh.

She waves her fork at him. "You do that just fine on your own."

"So, what are you doing in Miami if you aren't going to school?"

Her gaze drops to her uneaten food, and she avoids eye contact with me as she answers, "I'm not sure what I want to study, so I'm just taking some time for myself right now."

Voices grow at the other end of the table, catching our attention before Brody announces, "Who's down for going out?"

Trent tosses his napkin onto the table. "I'm in."

"Where are we going?" another one of the guys asks.

"We're in Boca. Let's find a club or something and celebrate."

Micah scoots his chair back. "Count me out."

"Yeah, me too. I'm tired," Ady says, finally giving that uneaten piece of broccoli a rest.

"You two suck," Trent complains and then looks my way. "You bailing too?"

"Not a chance."

With that, Trent stands and takes my hand, practically pulling me out of my seat before we all head out and pile into Brody's car. Several of us squeeze into the back seat, and I have to bite my bottom lip to control my smile when Trent slips his arm around my shoulders. I know there's nothing behind the gesture and that he only did it because we're all cramped back here, but I foolishly pretend for a moment there's something more behind it.

Again, Trent pulls out his pen, but when he taps the button to turn it on, he huffs, "Shit, the battery is dead."

I unzip my clutch and pull out my own pen, tap the button, and watch Trent's smile grow when the green light flashes.

"I think I just fell in love." He then snatches the pen and takes a hit.

"With me or the pot?"

It takes a few seconds of him holding in the vapor before he hands the pen back to me and answers, "The pot. Always the pot." He tightens his arm around my shoulders and presses a kiss to the side of my head.

I take two long pulls to tame the damn butterflies he just set off, settle back into his hold, and get stoned.

I'm light and free from emotion when we file into the dimly lit club. Loud music thumps so hard it vibrates through my bones, and I almost miss when the girl behind the counter slips a black bracelet on Trent's wrist.

"How'd you get that?" I yell over the music as I hold up my hand, showing him the giant X written in Sharpie on the back of it, marking me as under twenty-one.

He smiles, and I melt, all the while cursing him for being so perfect. Perfect lips, perfect teeth, perfect tan, and perfectly imperfect eyes. He then takes my hand and leads me over to the bar so he can order two shots, slipping me one when the bartender isn't looking. We throw back the vodka, which only enhances my high.

Music screams through my head as lights flash from all around, and the next thing I know, I'm on the dance floor. My arms fly above me, and I can't even tell if I'm dancing on beat—not that I care because when I spin around, Trent is right there.

He even dances perfectly.

I sway a little too far back, and he grabs my wrists and pulls them around his neck, which is damp with sweat. Suddenly, all the emotions I tried to dull with the weed come barreling down on me. With his hands on my hips, we move to the rhythm of the song within a sea of people.

I'm so far outside of myself, wondering what it is about this asshole of a guy that I'm so drawn to. Guys rarely catch my eye, but somehow, this one has me hooked, and I don't know why.

His thumb comes to my forehead, and he drags it lightly along my hairline, but it isn't until he slips it into his mouth that I realize he's tasting my sweat.

Holy shit, that's hot!

He tugs me in closer, and as we continue to move, his hands start to roam. I can't deny how good it feels, and I so want to get lost in his touch, but then a flash of sobriety strikes out of nowhere.

This guy only wants to get laid.

I'm not a fuck and duck type of girl—I'm not a prude, but I'm also not that.

"I'm getting lightheaded," I lie as I push away from him, feeling super uncomfortable about where this is going.

"What's wrong?"

"I think I got too much sun," I mutter, stepping back. When I do, I bump into the girl behind me. "Sorry."

"It was cloudy all day," Trent calls out while I start making my way through the crowd.

"Clouds are water vapor, not shields," I shout back, appalled that I let him get that close to me when clearly he only has one thing on his mind.

Maybe I'm overreacting, but my instincts are telling me I'm not.

The last thing I need to be doing is acting like the bunnies I despise.

Three

KATE

"DAD TOTALLY EMBARRASSED ME," AUDRINA COMPLAINS OVER the phone as I straighten my hair. "I was literally only thirty minutes past my curfew. You should have heard him. He laid into me right in front of Zach."

"You know how Mom and Dad are. They used to do the same thing to me."

"It was the first time I was late," she stresses.

"You don't have to convince me. But try to see it from Dad's point of view. He's a cop and he sees a lot of bad things," I explain. "Try to go easy on him. He's only trying to protect you."

"I was with Zach."

"That doesn't help, knowing his daughter is out late with some guy. I mean, come on. Can you blame him for being worried?"

"Oh my God. Are you serious? It isn't like that at all."

I unplug my flat iron, grab my cell, and head into my bedroom to change clothes. "So, what is it like between the two of you? Are you guys serious?"

"Ahhh," she exhales, and I know that if I had her on FaceTime instead of speakerphone, I would be able to see the love-struck, dreamy-eyes look on her face. "He is so hot."

I laugh. "Is that the only reason you're dating him?"

"No," she defends and then goes on to tell me about how sweet he is and how he slips cute little notes in her locker. She gushes on and on, which isn't surprising, and I've started to tune her out when she asks, "Do you think you can talk to Dad? This weekend is Stacy's sweet sixteen party, and I'm grounded."

"If I do, then he will know you called me after he grounded you from the phone."

"It's like I'm in prison."

"Far from it." I shrug on a flowy top and slip into a pair of sandals. "I'll talk to him tomorrow, but I can't make any promises."

"What are you going to say?"

"I don't know. I have to think about it, but I gotta run. I'm meeting a friend for dinner."

"Don't forget."

"I won't."

After we hang up, I head into the living room where Piper and her big sister from her sorority are hanging out. She tried talking me into attending rush week, but the whole sorority thing didn't appeal to me at all. Piper, on the other hand, loves Greek life.

"You look nice," she remarks as I grab my purse from the kitchen island. "You have a date I don't know about?"

"Please," I say with a roll of my eyes. "I'm grabbing dinner with Ady."

"Ady?"

"The girl I told you I met last month at the competition."

She doesn't respond as she and her friend focus on their craft.

"What are you even making?"

"Outfits for the eighties-themed mixer," her friend says as she holds up her T-shirt, which is covered in bright neon puff paint.

"Nice." The shirts they're so excited about are hideous. "I'll catch you later."

I take the elevator down to the parking garage, hop into my hatchback, and head over to Ady's condo, which also happens to be Trent's as well. I had no clue she lived with him and Micah until I went over there the other week. I was shocked to see him, but I was also secretly happy. It's the reason I put a little more effort into my look tonight, but I would never admit that to anyone.

For his part, it seems he has me stuck in the friend zone. He hangs out with Brody a lot, so he's always around when we all hit the water, and since I've been spending time with Ady, Trent and I are starting to form a decent friendship.

Before I get out of the car, I check my face in the rearview mirror one last time. When I arrive at their unit and knock on the door, I'm greeted with Trent yelling, "It's open!"

Inside, I find him sitting on the couch with a textbook on his lap. He doesn't look up to acknowledge me as he taps his highlighter against his knee.

"Everything okay?"

"Yeah," he murmurs absentmindedly without even glancing in my direction.

His distractedness is a letdown. I know better than to think Trent, from what little I know about him, would even notice the extra effort I put into my appearance. It was stupid to even think that he would, but I did it anyway.

"Ady, come on," I call out, wanting to leave, and head toward the hallway. Ady is staring into Micah's room, and it doesn't seem as if she heard me. "You ready?"

"Yeah." She pulls herself away from his door, and when she walks into the living room, she looks curiously at Trent. "What are you doing?"

"Studying."

She cracks a smile. "Have you ever done that before?" she teases, but Trent isn't amused.

He drops the book onto the coffee table and tosses his highlighter to the floor. "Shit's got me stressed out."

"What are you talking about? Nothing stresses you out," she says.

"My mom has been up my ass lately about her expectations of decent grades."

"Macroeconomics," I read aloud when I pick up the book. "Who do you have?"

He finally looks at me when he answers, "Carson. Tuesday and Thursday. Why?"

I hand the book to him. "I have Carson Monday, Wednesday, and Friday," I mention and take this opportunity to add, "So, if you need help . . ."

"You actually understand this?"

"Enough to be managing a B."

"I have a C . . . barely," he says while thrusting an aggravating hand through his hair. "Can you stop by tomorrow morning? I don't have class until noon."

The invitation strikes a match in my chest, and I forcibly hold back the smile that's tugging on my lips. "Nine?"

He nods, barely looking my way, and then heads into the kitchen with a casual, "Cool," before he opens the fridge.

And just like that, the flame in my chest snuffs, and no more do I have to fight my smile because now all I am is annoyed.

"Let's go." Ady sighs, pushing me toward the door, well-aware of the tension.

I haven't mentioned anything about Trent to anyone aside from Ady. She didn't even ask, she just knew. Apparently, I wasn't hiding my crush very well, and she warned me that he isn't the least bit interested in getting involved in a relationship with anyone. It should've deterred me, I wish it had, but it hasn't and neither has being friend zoned.

There's nothing worse than pining over a guy who isn't emotionally available. Yet, here I am, pining even though I am the one who walked away from him in Boca.

"You're not actually going to tutor him, are you?" Ady asks as we drive to Lulu's for dinner.

I roll to a stop when I hit a red light and flick on the blinker. "Why not?"

From my peripheral, I catch her giving me a knowing side eye.

"What?"

"Nothing," she says. "I just don't want you to get any unrealistic expectations."

"It's just a study session, that's all."

"Uh-huh, right," she snarks, which has me chuckling under my breath.

It's been nice hanging out with Ady lately. She's so different from Piper and most of the girls around here. She isn't one to talk a lot about herself or what is clearly going on between her and Micah. In fact, she isn't much of a talker at all, at least not about anything that's too personal.

It isn't long before we arrive at the restaurant. We order our dinner and chat about the upcoming spring semester, but when curiosity gets the better of me, I can't help myself from asking, "So, what's up with you and Micah?"

Her eyes lift to mine. "What do you mean?"

"Oh, come on." It is so obvious that Micah has a thing for her.

"What?"

"You're kidding me, right? Tell me you aren't blind to how he looks at you."

"Oh my god. No," she squeaks. "It isn't like that at all. Like, *at all,* at all." I shoot her an unconvinced glare. "I'm serious. We're just good friends. And if he's giving me looks, it's only looks of concern."

"Concern?"

"I used to date his best friend," she reveals. "We broke up right before I moved here."

"So, he's your shoulder to cry on?"

She shrugs off my comment. "Does it look like I'm crying on anyone's shoulder?"

She's delusional, and I'm not buying it. The two of them are so close that, had I not known better, I would assume they were an official couple.

"Well," I say as I pick up my fork and pierce an asparagus spear, "it would be an attractive shoulder to cry on. You know? If you ever do decide you need a good cry."

Four

KATE

With clammy palms, I raise my hand to the door and knock.

I'm nervous.

It's stupid. I've been over here numerous times since meeting Ady, but this is the first time I'm here for someone else.

"Hey, girl," Ady says as she opens the door, and I step in.

"What are you up to?" I ask, noticing that she's completely pulled together at nine AM.

"Heading out with Micah. He has some errands to run, so I figured I'd tag along with him."

"Oh."

Her brows cinch slightly with curiosity, and I'm sure she can tell I'm a little flustered. Okay, a lot flustered. I assumed she'd be here the whole time considering she's pretty much a homebody.

"Stop gabbing," Trent says from where he's sitting in the living room with his books already open. "I need to leave in a couple of hours, and you have to teach me all this shit before my quiz today."

For the second time in as many days, Trent manages to crush my hopeful nerves and drag my mood straight into a huge pile of annoyance.

Ady giggles with a sing-song, "Have fun."

"Right."

Micah emerges from his room and the two of them head out as I make my way over to sit next to Trent on the couch.

"The quiz is easy, by the way."

"You already took it?"

"Yeah. Yesterday before I came over here."

He smiles. "Perfect. You remember the questions?"

"I thought I was here to tutor you, not help you cheat."

"Nothing is going to help my grade more than you giving me the answers."

I take his textbook and drop it onto his lap, saying, "I don't think so," before pulling my text out from my backpack.

"Seriously?"

"Yeah, seriously, Trent. I'm not just going to give you all the answers."

He flips his book open with feigned annoyance.

"So, what do you need help with?"

"Everything."

"Okay. How about we start with consumer sovereignty?" We both turn to that section in the chapter, and I quickly explain how consumers are the ones who influence production decisions. We go through a few paragraphs, and I point out the key terms he'll need to know for the quiz. If he notices my specificity of those terms, he doesn't show it. When I have him read over a section so I can explain a command economy, I find myself completely distracted. For the first time, I see him in a different light—serious. I catch myself gazing his way, noticing how his bottom lip twitches when he's concentrating. I wonder if he's aware that he does this or if it's an absentminded tick.

I shouldn't be looking at him like this. It wasn't but last week when we were all surfing at the beach that I watched him pick up a bunny right in front of me. I'd be lying if I said it didn't burn, but I played nonchalant since I'd pretty much shot him down that night in the club and hadn't given him any reason to think I'd changed my stance since.

A lock of his over-grown hair falls down onto his forehead, and when he flicks his head to sweep it back, he catches me watching him and smirks.

"Like what you see?" he teases, but I just let out a huff of annoyance.

"Are you done reading?"

"I can slow down if you want to look more."

His cocky smile melts my bones and strengthens my irritation. "Are you always like this?"

"Like what?"

I could ask, but why bother? I already know his answer. "Never mind."

"I'm serious . . ." He scoots closer to me and slips his arm around my shoulders. "You know you want to give me the answers."

Having him this close to me, touching me, has me flustered. On one hand, I want this, but on the other, I don't because it's insincere at best—he's only doing it to get the answers for the quiz.

"We could do something else with this time instead of studying."

"Really?" I exclaim, taking his arm and flinging it off me. "Is that all you think about?"

He laughs. "Relax. I figured we could have some fun if you wanted to. Apparently, you don't, so no foul, man."

My look narrows to a glare. I hate that he's so flippant.

"Do girls actually fall for . . ." I wag my hand in front of him, "*this*?"

His brows cinch. "Dude! Why you gotta be so insulting?"

"*Me*? I don't think so. You're the insulting one, assuming I'm a low-moral girl who'll put out at the drop of hat."

"Nice backhanded insult." He shoots me a wink. "Just give me a chance, and I'll show you my morals."

I grab one of the pillows on the couch and smack him with it, but he's quick to yank it out of my hands, grab my wrist, and pull me toward him.

A weak piece of me is screaming for him to kiss me. His lips are close enough that it wouldn't take much effort at all, but he kills it when he snarks, "I'd be the best you've ever had."

I push him away. "God, you are so full of yourself."

His laughter grows, and it's hard to tell if he's just kidding around or if he's an actual egotistical douche. If only he weren't so damn hot, it would make it easier to slap him in the latter category.

"You can consider me off limits."

"You sure about that?"

No.

"Completely."

He settles into the couch and grabs his text. "That's a shame."

It really is.

I shake my head and go back to the book, explaining the section he just read before moving on to the next, which covers market economies.

As he reads, I attempt to compartmentalize the swarm of emotions flitting through me. I'm entirely distracted, and I can't seem to pull myself together. Next thing I know, I'm again sneaking glances his way while he studies.

"None of this shit makes sense," he says after a while. "I mean, who the hell even cares about this stuff?"

"You need to care if you want to pass."

"Or you can just slip me the answers."

"Not a chance."

With a huff, he slacks back into the couch and starts to read through the next section. I watch as his eyes skitter across the pages, mesmerized by the conflicting colors. I drift back to last month at the dance club. When I think about that night, I can't help but wonder what our relationship would look like today if we had hooked up. Even though I am so far from a one-night-stand girl, I find myself imagining what it would be like to be with him in that way. It's a lustful thought that I shouldn't even entertain, but I keep doing it.

The next hour passes, and I manage to catch him up on the chapter, but just barely. I take the time alone with him for what it's worth, which for him, probably isn't anything more than him wanting to improve his grade.

Crushes suck.

As we're going through the review questions at the end of the chapter, his cell phone rings. He picks it up, reads the screen, and stands. "I got to take this. Give me a second."

He walks to his bedroom, which is in earshot of the living room, and kicks the door shut. It doesn't latch closed, so I can still hear his voice as he asks, "What's going on?"

I shouldn't eavesdrop, but when he tells the person on the other end, "Calm down. Just tell me what happened," my curiosity piques.

He's quiet for a moment, and then his voice raises in anger. "He did what?"

He's clearly pissed, and I'm clearly intruding on a private conversation, but it feels weird to just up and leave. Whomever he's talking to is upset. Trent attempts to calm the person down, asking questions that make no sense to me as I try to dissect what the conversation is even about.

Uncomfortably, I sit, because to do anything else would only feel more awkward.

"How did you not know?" he asks, followed by a short pause before adding, "He's a piece of shit." Another pause. "No! He is. I don't even know why you're defending him."

This stern side is yet another facet of him I hadn't come across before this morning, and I wish I could see his expression. I bet his eyes would be bright with anger.

"Do you need me? Just say the word, and I'm there."

Beneath my unease lays jealousy, which is an emotion I've become all too familiar with since meeting Trent. I have no idea who he's talking to, but there is a fierce protectiveness in his tone that is generally only afforded to people you care deeply for. What is it about this person that has him so concerned and attentive the way I wish he would be with me?

I shake the thought away, but it doesn't go far when I realize that he's ended the conversation. There's nothing but silence coming from his bedroom. I wait for him to reappear, but he doesn't.

Tension mounts, and a big part of me considers bailing. It's the same pull that keeps me coming around that's telling me I should stay.

I give him a few more minutes, and when he doesn't return, I hesitantly stand and walk toward his room. He's sitting on the edge of his bed, hunched over with his head hanging down and his hands wringing. I move so that I'm standing just inside the threshold, and he looks up.

There's emotion etched all over his face. I freeze, unsure of what to say, because whatever that was all about has him upset.

When I open my mouth to speak, he cuts me off with a bleak, "You should probably go."

I want to ask him if everything is all right, but questioning him seems like an overstep. We tease and push each other's buttons, we don't do seriousness.

"Are you sure?" I ask, hoping that maybe I'm wrong about him and that we could possibly have a meaningful conversation, but he shoots me down.

"I didn't stutter," he responds coarsely.

The sharpness of his words stuns me for a moment, but that quickly fades when I realize that he's lashing out at me because he's upset. That I understand, so without another word, I nod and duck out of his room, gather all my belongings, and leave.

While I'm driving back home, he's heavy on my mind as I consider what happened to cause his mood to take such a sudden shift. The reasons could be infinite, so I give up trying to figure them out. If he wanted me to know, he would've told me.

I try to not take him telling me to leave personally, but the sting is there regardless. It's pathetic that I would even assume he would confide in me. I shouldn't have even entertained that idea.

I know better.

I feel like a fool as I head to my condo, and when I walk through the door, I toss my backpack on the floor and fall onto the couch.

"What's wrong with you?" Piper asks from the kitchen.

"Boys suck."

"Tell me about it." She walks into the room with a bag of chips and sits on the sofa next to me. "Who's the boy?" she asks before shoving a chip into her mouth.

"No one important."

"If he isn't important, then why are you so upset?"

"I'm not upset."

"Oh-kay," she responds unbelieving, dragging out the word.

"I'm pissed," I clarify. "I mean, why are they all such single-minded pricks?"

"Because they just are. Since when do you care about guys?"

"I don't," I retort.

She pops another chip into her mouth as she stares curiously at me. "Does this have something to with Derek?"

"God, no!" I haven't spoken to—or even thought twice about—my ex-boyfriend who dumped me right before high school graduation.

"You sure?"

"Yeah, I'm sure."

Piper knows that Derek didn't leave me heartbroken—he left me pissed off.

I grab the bag of chips, shove a handful into my mouth, and chomp down in frustration.

"If you won't tell me who the loser is, will you at least tell me what happened?"

"Nothing. That's the problem. I'm too chicken shit to tell him that I like him."

"Seriously?"

"What?" I exclaim as she gawks at me.

She swipes the bag from my hands and tosses it onto the coffee table. "Look, I know you have no experience with guys—"

"Gee, thanks."

"I didn't mean that to be bitchy, I'm just saying, take it from me . . . guys are dumb. Like, *stupid* dumb. You literally have to spell things out for them," she says. "How is this guy supposed to know that you like him if you've never told him?"

"Honestly, he's not even worth telling."

"Well, if he isn't worth telling, then he isn't worth you being upset over."

Five

TRENT

"THIS IS THE LAST ONE," MY MOM SAYS AS SHE HOISTS A BOX OF Christmas decorations up to me.

"Good, because it's hotter than the devil's dick up here."

"Trent! Language!"

I stack the box next to the others in the corner of the attic before crawling out and stepping down the ladder into the garage.

"Thank you so much, honey."

Taking the hem of my T-shirt, I wipe the sweat from my forehead.

"I don't know what I would do without you."

We head back into the house where the AC is blasting, and I flop down onto one of the chairs in the living room. "You're a chump, you know that?" I say to Garrett, my older brother, who's kicked back on the couch.

"What's got your panties in a wad?"

"I could've used your help. I was sweating my balls off up in that attic."

Garrett laughs, and I chuck a pillow at his head.

"Boys," my mother nags as she walks into the room.

"Don't look at me. Trent's the tulip here."

31

"Eat dick."

"Ugh." Mom groans as she swats at my brother's legs. "Sit up and make room for me."

My mother has the patience of a saint, and I'm surprised with how well she's been holding herself together with everything she's been going through with Richard, my stepdad. When she called me a month ago to tell me she'd found out about his gambling addiction, I was just as shocked as she was. Apparently, he'd admitted to lying about their finances to cover for the debt he got himself into. On top of that, he drained the bank accounts, stole the stones out of several pieces of her jewelry, and pawned them for cash. He even had the balls to swap them for fake ones so she wouldn't find out, but eventually she did.

I love my mother more than anything, but I'm pissed that she had no clue about what he was doing. She married him and then just turned all the finances over to him without bothering to be involved at all.

He's now renting an apartment up north in Carollwood, which is only twenty minutes from us, but I haven't seen him since I've been home for Christmas break. As soon as I was done with my last final, I drove here to be with her. The last thing I wanted was for her to be alone in this big house.

I saw how hard it was on her when Garrett moved out. The woman moped around for a couple of weeks like the kid died or something. And then six months ago, when I left for Miami, she was even worse. And now her husband is gone. She holds herself together pretty well for the most part, but I've caught her crying a few times.

"I really do appreciate all of your help around the house," she says to me and Garrett. "I guess I never realized how much Richard did."

"You're going to be fine, Mom," Garrett tells her, and I know the smile she's giving him is pasted on for his sake.

She doesn't want us to worry about her, but we are worried.

"Maybe I shouldn't have been so quick to throw him out," she says.

"Fuck that."

"Garrett!"

"He's right, Mom. That guy turned out to be a total taint," I tell her, irritated that she would even second-guess her decision to kick him out.

Her teary eyes drop, sending a pang through my chest, and I refrain from saying anything else that might upset her. If there's one person in this world I have a soft spot for, it's her. We've always been close. Between her career as a pediatrician and her volunteer work with the Junior League, she never missed a single little league or lacrosse game. She was always there for my brother and me when we were growing up, and even though the roll of stepdad has been a revolving door since my dad left when I was five years old, her presence never wavered. To see her, time and time again, struggling to pick up the pieces of her life is a hard thing to watch.

Garrett gives my mother's knee a reassuring squeeze. "You did the right thing."

She nods reluctantly before looking over at me, and I agree, saying, "He's right. That guy lied and stole from you."

She releases a defeated sigh before standing and making her way outside.

"Look, I didn't want to say anything in front of Mom," Garrett says. "But I talked to Richard last night."

"What did he say?"

"Not much. We didn't get into anything serious, but he doesn't sound good, man."

"That's his fucking problem, not ours."

His shoulders slacken. "Yeah, I know," he mutters.

Neither of us wants to admit that the disintegration of another marriage sucks ass, but I need to get some space.

"Where are you going?" he questions when I stand and start walking toward the stairs.

"I'm going to go skimming at Indian Rocks." I head upstairs, throw on my swim trunks, and grab my skimboard. I desperately need to get out of this house. It's way too tense.

Before I hit the front door, I text Micah.

Me: Heading to Indian Rocks. You down?
Micah: Yeah.
Me: I'll come pick you up.

It takes only a handful of minutes before I'm passing over the small bridge that leads to the gated community on Harbour Island where his parents live. Rolling in front of the drive, I lie on the horn, and a few moments later, Micah comes out with his board tucked under his arm.

"Let's do this," he says when he jumps into the passenger seat of my SUV.

With the sunroof and windows open, we cruise across the Gandy bridge and over to Indian Rocks beach. The humidity is unusually thick for this time of year, and it's no surprise that the ocean water is hotter than normal—not that the gulf waters really ever get cold like they do in Miami.

"Look at this flat, shit," Micah drones.

"We're skimming, little bitch," I shout as I run past him, drop my board, and jump on, riding the sliver of water that rolls up the shore.

We spend the next hour or so throwing down tricks and

skimming the swashes that rush up the sand. The beach is pretty much ours with only a few people scattered about, which is why I love it here. No tourists flock to this area; it's all locals.

"Are we calling it?" I ask when Micah grabs his board.

"Yeah, man. I need a breather."

When we sit in the sand and Micah tosses me a bottle of water from his backpack, he asks, "Is that Henley?"

"Where?"

"Over there," he says, pointing to the chick I couldn't get rid of after we hooked up last year.

"Fuck." I breath the curse, praying to the gods above that she doesn't see me. "Who knew she'd turn into a crazy barnacle?"

Micah laughs. He knows the nightmare she put me through. The girl kept texting and calling, blowing up my damn phone and not taking the hint, which wasn't even a hint. I flat-out told her that I wasn't interested in anything other than having fun. I eventually had to block her.

"Should we warn the guy she's talking to?" he says under a chuckle.

I shake my head. "Not my problem, bruh. But speaking of chicks, what's going on with you and Ady?"

"Nothing, man. The girl is still completely hung up on her ex."

"Still?"

He shrugs.

"So, are you going to tell her that you're smacked?"

"I'm not fucking smacked," he defends, but it's bullshit.

"Dude, don't even try to deny the fact that you've had a thing for her ever since she moved here junior year."

"Whatever, man." He brushes it off before chugging his water and turning the damn table on me. "And what about Kate?"

"What about her?"

"You guys are hanging out all the time. What's up with that?"

"Nothing's up."

"Your eyes are turning brown." He laughs.

"Fuck off." Truth is, it doesn't matter how I feel about anyone. I'm not into commitment. It isn't my thing. I'm down for fun. The last thing I want is drama from a relationship. Never had one, and I'm not interested in starting one. "We're friends, man."

"Are you sure that's all?"

"Yeah, she's turned me down a few times, so I gave up."

I still see the way she looks at me when she thinks I'm not paying attention, but I can't read her beyond that. Every advance I make, she pushes me away. Most of the time, she seems annoyed with me, but I've hung out with her enough to know she's a chill girl. Fucking her would only ruin our friendship. Since we run in the same circle, it would wind up creating tension because she's made it clear that she isn't into anything casual.

"Why do you keep her around then?"

"It's kind of hard not to when she's friends with Ady and is always at our place. Plus, she's good friends with Brody and the whole crew," I defend, but I can tell he isn't buying it.

Yeah, the chick is hot, a surfer, and mellow—the perfect package. I like that it's uncomplicated and easy.

"Has Ady said anything to you?"

I release a breathy chuckle. "Ady would have my meat kiwis in a blender if I did anything with Kate."

We both laugh because it's the truth. Ady has become a little sister of sorts, and she has no problem voicing her opinions about me. Plus, after watching how much she's struggled to make girlfriends after she moved to Florida from Texas, I don't want to be the cause of ruining what appears to be a solid friendship between the two of them. It's also evident that Kate is helping Ady through whatever Kason did to her, which is another reason why it would be a terrible idea to hook-up with her.

"Enough shit," he says, changing the topic. "How's everything with your mom?"

"Not good."

"Have you talked to your stepdad since you've been home?"

"Hell no."

Despite all the shitty men my mom has been with throughout the years, I kind of liked Richard. But him pissing away all the money and lying to my mom about it is fucked up. That dude can eat ass shit for the rest of his life as far as I'm concerned.

"I'm sorry, man," he says. "Shit sucks."

"Tell me about it."

And just like that, the pang in my chest returns.

Six

KATE

After a month off for Christmas break, it feels good to be back at school. Not that I didn't enjoy my time at home, but tensions were making me want to get back to Miami. Audrina hasn't been getting along so well with our parents lately. I know it's just her age. She wants to be treated like an adult when she is still a kid and she doesn't know how to navigate it so she lashes out. But she has a boyfriend now, so it's no surprise that all she wants to do is spend time with him.

"Kate," someone hollers across the bustling lawn, which is lined in pristine palm trees, as I'm making my way across campus to my communications class.

When I turn, Kylie is rushing my way. "Hey, what's up?"

"Nothing," she says as she catches up with me. "You heading to class?"

"Yeah, but I have a few minutes. How are you feeling this morning?"

"Like utter crap."

I met Kylie last semester. The two of us don't hang out much, but she was in my English Lit class last year and she always seems to be at all the parties I go to with Brody and Trent, including the one last night.

"Well, at least you don't look like crap."

She laughs. "Thanks."

"How's Jenna feeling?" I ask of her roommate. "She was so crazy last night."

"She should be feeling on top of the world," Kylie says with a sly grin as she pulls her cell phone out of her backpack. "I have to show you this guy she hooked up with last night."

When she hands the phone over to show me a picture of the guy in question, my stomach sinks.

"How do you know they hooked up?"

"Because I could hear them," she says. "Isn't he hot? I snuck the picture as he was leaving this morning."

I nod as I look at the photo of Trent before passing the phone back to her. "Yeah," I agree while faking a painful smile. "I, um, I've got to run, but I'll catch up with you later."

"Sounds good."

There's a tightening in my chest as I rush off to my class. It isn't that I'm shocked he hooked up with Jenna—he does this all the time—but to have it right in front of my face hurts.

I like Trent. I like him way more than I should, and I just wish he weren't so unavailable. It's stupid, I get it, but knowing he hooked up with Jenna last night makes me want to cry. With each step, my heart hurts a bit more, and I have to get this off my chest, so I pull out my phone and text Ady.

Me: Trent is an asshole!

When I walk into my communications class and find a seat, I check my phone to see if she's responded, but she hasn't. With frustrations swarming, I silently groan when the professor walks in and I'm forced to shut my cell off and spend the next hour listening as he reads through the syllabus.

It's hard to sit still when my mind is somewhere else. I

consider talking to Piper about all this but I feel pathetic as it is. Plus, we've been drifting anyways. Even though we live together, I rarely see her because she's constantly at the sorority house with all of her friends that I'm not a part of.

I slump back into my desk and count the minutes until class is over. My whole mood just sucks now, and when we're dismissed, I shove the syllabus into my bag, turn my phone on, and file out of the room with everyone else.

Ady: Why? What happened?
Me: Are you at the condo?

As I make my way to my next class, I wait for her to text back, but nothing comes. So, I switch my phone to silent and shove it into my bag.

I'm completely distracted by my own thoughts as I sit through my marketing class. Again, it's nothing more than listening to the professor drone over the syllabus, so when my phone vibrates from my backpack, which is sitting next to my feet, I don't feel guilty when I pull it out and check the message.

Ady: No. I'm on campus waiting for my class to start.

With fifteen minutes left, I duck out early and text her back.

Me: Thank God! I'm here, too. How long until your next class?
Ady: An hour.
Me: Where are you? I need to talk.
Ady: In front of the Cox building.
Me: On my way.

Picking up my pace, I hustle across campus and find her sitting on the grass near a palm tree.

"What's going on?" she asks.

With an aggravated sigh, I toss my bag to the ground and sit next to her. "I swore I'd never be this girl."

Ady raises a brow in curiosity.

I grab a wad of grass and rip it out of the ground before saying, "I found out that Trent slept with my friend's roommate. And before you say anything, I know I'm being stupid . . . but still . . ."

"You aren't being stupid," she tells me, but we both know that this is a pointless crush.

"I am, and I hate that I'm letting this crap get to me." I continue picking blades of grass, and when she shakes her head, I add, "I'm serious, I'm *so* not the girl who obsesses over a guy."

And that's the truth. Never has anyone captured my attention like Trent, and he did it without even trying. I don't have a clue what it is about him that has me so crazy. He's nothing like my ex. Heck, he's nothing like any guy I've ever met.

"Has he always been this way?"

Ady nods. "He means well, and I promise you, he isn't a bad guy," she tells me. "He's just a free spirit and does his best not to lead girls on. I've only ever seen him be upfront with that."

"I get it." And I do. It's obvious that he's just into chick surfing. It isn't like he's ever hid that about himself. "I just . . . I really like him, and I'm stuck in the damn friend zone."

"I know you like him, but I assure you that you're better off having him as a friend. He's too into his own thing to make a good boyfriend, and you're too good to sell yourself short just to get the satisfaction of hooking up with him. That isn't who you are anyway."

When she says this, I yank out a wad of grass and toss it out in front of me. With jealousy over Jenna and him having sex roiling through me, I question if Ady is correct in her assumption of who I am. Maybe I would sell myself short for a night with Trent.

No. I do not want to be a hit-and-run girl.

"Don't you ever tell anyone that I'm desperately crushing on a guy like this. It's majorly embarrassing."

She laughs. "Your secret's safe with me."

"Enough about me, how was your break?"

"Good," she says. "My mom came here and we celebrated Christmas at the condo."

"Why didn't you go back home to Tampa?"

She shrugs. "I thought Miami would be fun. You know, do something new."

"This doesn't have anything to do with your ex, does it?"

Something shifts in her eyes a second before she says, "No."

I've struck a chord with her, the same chord I seem to strike every time I mention her ex. She clearly doesn't want to talk about him; heck, I don't even know his name. But with how much I've opened up to her about all the Trent stuff, I wish she would do the same, so I test the waters and ask, "What happened between the two of you anyway?"

"Nothing," she quickly responds. "We just . . . we just didn't work out."

"Did you want it to work out?"

"Of course I did."

Her eyes fall, and now it's her who begins picking nervously at the grass.

"I'm sorry. If you don't want to talk about it just tell me."

"I don't want to talk about it," she says thickly, and I feel bad for prying.

"I won't ask any more about it. But if you ever want to talk . . ."

She nods, takes a hard swallow, and says, "I'm just trying to move forward without looking back."

Giving her an encouraging smile, I let it drop but allow the questions to linger in my own thoughts. She moved here nearly three months ago, so for her to still be this emotional over a high school boyfriend is strange. It doesn't add up to me, but everyone is different, I guess.

As I head in to my third and final class for the day, I feel better about the whole Trent thing. Ady is right; Trent isn't a bad guy, so I need to stop being pissed at him just because I wish he acted differently. It kind of makes me want to laugh. I like him for who he is, yet here I am, trying to change him to make him something he isn't.

I do what I can to shake it off as I take a seat toward the back of the stadium lecture hall and settle in for another boring syllabus review.

"Hell yeah!"

Oh, no.

Trent smiles down at me before taking the seat to my left.

"What are you doing?"

"What's it look like I'm doing?" he remarks as he gets cozy. "Were you saving this spot for someone?"

"What if I was?"

He stares into my eyes, effortlessly melting my irritation. The thaw only lasts a split second before he cocks a grin, knowing damn well I'm not saving the seat for anyone.

"Don't think that just because you're sitting next to me that I'm going to let you cheat off my work."

"I'm a whiz at this shit," he states concededly. "The only one you need to be worried about cheating is yourself."

"You're annoying."

"You're always so aggressive," he says before leaning in to me and whispering, "It's a turn on."

Shoving his shoulder, I push him away.

A part of me wants to ask him about Jenna to try to make him feel like shit for sleeping with her, but I know he won't. I doubt there's anything I could do that would get under his skin like he's gotten under mine. It's an ever-constant irk I wish would go away, and now that we share this class, I'm forced to endure its torture for the rest of the semester. With that being said, I can either be miserable or do what I can to make the best of it.

I choose the latter.

"How was your time back home?" I ask.

"It was chill," he responds. "What about you?"

"It was good."

Nothing else is said as we wait in awkward silence for class to start, but after a while, he surprises me when he says, "By the way. I didn't get a chance to apologize to you before you left for break."

"Apologize?"

"The way I treated you when you were helping me with my economics," he explains. "Sorry I was a prick to you."

I'm shocked that he's even addressing this after a month. Sure, I was pissed and hurt with how he'd just kind of dismissed me, but it didn't take long for me to let it go. I just didn't expect that he was still hanging on to it.

"It's okay. Don't worry about it."

He gives an appreciative nod.

"I hope everything is okay with whatever that situation was."

"Everything's cool."

Before I can say anything else, I catch Jenna from the corner of my eye as she walks in. I look at Trent to see his reaction, but he doesn't notice her at all as she glances our way. Suddenly, visions of the two of them together cloud my head, abrading my mood and tearing it back down.

She takes a seat a few rows down, and when Trent leans in and says something to me, she glares over her shoulder at us.

I quickly take my eyes off her and turn into Trent. "What?" I ask, too distracted to hear what he said.

"I still feel like shit from last night," he repeats.

"Maybe you shouldn't drink so much."

"Okay, Mom," he teases, causing me to chuckle under my breath, and when I look back at Jenna, she scowls before turning around.

When class begins, I grab my phone out of my bag, and without Trent noticing, I shoot a quick text to Jenna.

Me: It isn't what you think. He's roommates with one of my friends. That's all.

I watch her, and after a few seconds, she pulls out her phone and reads the message that's only a half-version of the truth. Her response is to drop her cell down into her bag and ignore me for the rest of class.

Seven

KATE

PULLING THE SLEEVES OF MY WETSUIT OVER MY ARMS, I LOOK OUT AT the ocean where the morning sun hangs just above.

"You ready?"

I give Brody a nod as I reach over my shoulder, yank up the zipper pull, and secure myself in my suit. "Let's go."

"Fuck yeah," Trent calls out as we grab our boards and head out into the chilly February water.

My dad called and woke me up at five o'clock when he was heading to work this morning to tell me that waves would be at a rare high this morning in Palm Beach. Because the swells are moving in the direction in which they are, they're able to refract around the Bahamas to give this beach a great day of surfing. When I called Brody to tell him, he was all in and invited Trent and Micah to join us. For whatever reason, Micah bailed, so it's just the three of us.

After jogging into the water, I hop belly first onto my board and paddle out, duck-diving through the breaks until I'm out in the lineup, where I stop and push myself to sitting. The rising sun pierces my eyes as I glance to Brody, who is on my left, and then to Trent, who is on my right. Like me, they are both waiting for the next set that's rolling in. We're far enough apart from one another that Brody has to holler for me to hear when he shouts, "Paddle!"

When I see the wave set, I turn around on my board, lie down, and dig my hands into the water before popping up. A rush of spray blasts my cheeks as I glide down the face and ride out the wave until I hit the closeout and kick out.

As I get ready to catch another ride, Trent shouts excitedly from a distance. I laugh, and when he catches my eye, he shoots me a shaka. Dipping the nose of my board beneath a break, I paddle out a little farther. With salt in my long brown hair and the warm breath of the morning sun on my face, I'm at peace. There was a time when I wanted to run away from the water and never come back, but I eventually came back. The ocean has always been my home through the good and bad.

This is the beach my father used to bring me to, and the one I continued to come to as I grew up and no longer needed him in the water with me. Although Miami is only a short hour and a half from my home, at times it feels like a world away.

As the sky grows brighter, the three of us continue to surf and enjoy the near-empty water. There are a few other people out here taking advantage of the swells, but there aren't so many that I have to worry about kooks dropping in on me.

Sitting on my board, I bob on the water like a buoy. As I stare down a ways and watch Brody, I find myself blinking against a few dark floaters in my vision. I shake my head and pinch my eyes shut, but when I open them, there are still dark spots.

"Not again," I whisper to myself as I close my eyes and press my palms against them, already feeling a dull band of throbbing across my forehead.

We've been out in the water for almost two hours, but I'm not ready to call it a day yet. So, I ignore the growing tension around my temples and set myself up to catch the next wave, and when I pop up, I ride it perfectly, pulling a couple of kick-backs as I do. It's when I hit the pocket that my vision darkens and blurs. The moment I whip my head, my foot slips and I lose my balance, falling off and clipping my head on the board before the wave crashes down and pulls me under. A spark of light flashes from behind my lids, taking me right back to the accident, and I panic as I try to find the surface.

My leash tangles around my other leg as I swim toward the surface, and when I finally break through, I find Brody behind the dense shadows that cloud my sight paddling my way.

"Kate," he hollers. "You okay?"

My heart pounds against my ribs while I attempt to pull myself onto my board. Another stabbing pain slices through my head, and I know I need to get out of the water and lie down.

Brody's hand clasps around my wrist, and he pulls me onto my board. "Is it your head again?"

"Yeah." I pant as I catch my breath.

"Here," he says, unfastening his leash and tossing it my way. "Hold on."

I grab the chord, and he starts paddling us back in as I tow from behind.

When we hit the shore, the two of us walk over to our bags, and I flop down onto the sand. Brody tosses me a water, and I guzzle it before pulling my knees to my chest and resting my head on them.

"What's going on?" Trent calls out, and when I look up, he's jogging our way with his board tucked under his arm.

My cheeks scorch with embarrassment, but the pain in my head forces me to close my eyes again.

"What happened?"

Before Brody can answer with the truth, I tell an easy lie. "Nothing. I just slipped and hit my head."

"You okay?"

"Yeah, I'll be fine."

"Kate," Brody says with concern in his eyes.

"I'm fine. No big deal," I stress right before another flame of agony spears its way through my head. My jaw clenches as I hiss through the pain, squeezing my eyes shut.

"We should get you home," Brody suggests before pulling his phone from his bag. "Fuck. It's already ten." He then looks to Trent and asks, "Would you mind taking her back?"

"What?" I question at the same time Trent agrees. "No," I say. "I don't want to leave my car here. It's too far."

"I'm going to be late for class, and this professor is a jackass who actually takes attendance. I can't be late."

"It's cool," Trent tells him. "Go ahead and get out of here."

"You sure, man?"

"Yeah."

"Okay, thanks," he tells Trent and then looks at me. "I'll call you later, okay?"

I give him a small smile, and he's out.

"Why don't you just take me to my parents' house? It's only twenty minutes from here. I'll pick up my car later when my dad gets off work."

"You sure?"

"Yeah, it's fine."

He offers me a hand up, and I take it, allowing him to pull me to my feet. The sudden shift is enough to blur my vision again. Hunching over, I grip my knees until the fog clears.

"Dude, how hard did you hit your head?"

"Let's just go."

He takes my board with his, and I sling my backpack over my shoulders as we walk to his SUV. The pain amplifies as he drives me to the house I grew up in, and by the time he pulls into the drive, I have a full-blown migraine.

"You okay walking in?"

"Yeah, thanks for the ride," I tell him as he watches me get out of the car. I can tell he's worried, but I brush it off because it's embarrassing to have people fuss over me.

Grabbing my board from the back of his SUV, I thank him again and then head up to the garage to punch in the code, but between the throbbing in my head and my speckled vision, I become dizzy and stumble in my step.

My board drops from under my arm, and in the next moment, Trent is out of the SUV with his hands around my arms, holding me up.

"What's the code?"

"Nine two one two," I tell him, wanting nothing more than to rinse the salt from my skin and lie down already.

The garage opens, and Trent gets me inside. As soon as I hit the foot of the stairs, I peel off my wetsuit, which was already shoved down to my waist, and kick it aside on the tile floor, leaving me in my bikini.

"Damn," Trent remarks, stretching out the word, and I'm quick to smack him.

"Shut up." When I start walking up the stairs toward my old bedroom, Trent picks up my wetsuit and follows me. "What do you think you're doing?"

"Making sure your ass doesn't fall down the stairs because you're walking around like a sloptart."

"A sloptart? Really?"

He laughs, and when I turn around to climb the rest of the stairs, I mumble, "You're such a dick," loud enough for him to hear.

"You mind if I change? I don't want to drive home like this."

When I hit the door to my room, I turn to look at him standing in his wetsuit, which is tugged down to his waist, and if I didn't feel so shitty, I might actually notice butterflies.

"Yeah, that's fine. I'm going to hop in the shower and rinse off. You can change in there," I say, pointing to the guest restroom.

"Sounds good. I'll just show myself out when I'm done." He walks down the hall with his backpack that has his dry clothes in it.

"Okay. Thanks for the ride," I tell him as I head into my room. I grab a T-shirt and a pair of athletic shorts from my dresser before I close the door to my en-suite bathroom.

Once I'm alone, I give in to the sharp pain. My eyes well with tears as I sit on the edge of the bathtub. With my head in my palms, I clench my teeth through the tremendous pounding in my head. It's been a few months since I've had one of these episodes, and I don't have my medicine on me. My pills are back at my condo, but I might have some in one of the drawers by the sink.

After riffling through them and coming up empty, I slip off my bikini, turn the bathroom lights off, and hop into the shower. I brace my hands against the wall and let the hot water pelt against my skin, doing what I can to focus on the sensation of the spray in an attempt to distract myself from the gnawing pain of my migraine.

Time fades, but I know enough of it has passed when the water turns cold and my fingertips have pruned. It's only then that I step out of the shower and slowly dry off and change. My movements aren't slow enough though, and the floaters return, obscuring my vision. As I lean over the sink, I stare into the mirror at the faint scar that runs just under my right brow where I had thirteen stitches.

The memory of that terrifying day causes another tear to slip down my already splotchy face. Backing away, I open the door and find Trent sitting on my bed.

"What are you still doing here?"

He scans my face and stands. "I heard you crying."

Heat creeps up my neck.

"I thought you might have a concussion or something, but when I went down to the garage to check out your board, I didn't see anything, not even a ding, so I know you couldn't have hit it that hard."

"I'm fine, I . . . I have a migraine."

"I just wanted to make sure everything was okay before I left."

His usual jokester mood has been exchanged for one that seems . . . sincere, which, for him, is completely foreign.

"All my medicine is back in Miami."

The corner of his mouth lifts into a subtle grin, and he walks over to his bag on the floor next to my dresser and pulls out a small vial.

"What's that?"

"Cannabis," he says. "It's just tinctured."

"I don't need to be getting blasted."

"Relax," he says as he steps over to me. "I'm not going to give you enough to get blasted." He unscrews the dropper. "Open your mouth and lift your tongue."

I do, and he squeezes out a few drops before dropping some in his mouth as well.

"I've only ever vaped or done edibles," I tell him as I walk over to the bed and sit.

"This is longer-lasting. You should like it."

"I need to lay my head down," I tell him. "Would you mind closing the blinds? The light is killing me."

I slip down on top of the covers as he moves around my room, putting the vial away and then turning my blinds closed.

He stops to look at a photo on my dresser and cracks a chuckle, teasing, "You look hot in braces."

"Why do you have to be an ass?" I mumble.

He laughs as he walks over to the bed and sits beside me. "No worries. I had them too."

My nerves kick up, but they don't feel like they should as the onset of my high starts to settle in. I close my eyes, sink into the dullness, and finally, I mellow out enough not to be in so much pain. When my equilibrium gets thrown off as if I'm on a slow-moving rollercoaster, I open my eyes.

"Feels good, right?"

I nod as all my muscles slacken.

We settle into a comfortable silence as both our highs take effect, and after a while, Trent lays his head on the pillow next to where I'm lying.

He lets go of a heavy sigh and then turns to look at me. "You feeling better?"

"A little."

"You always fake migraines to get guys into bed with you?"

A soft, airy laugh slips out of me. "My dad would have his gun on you if he saw you in my bed."

Trent quirks a nervous brow.

"He's a cop."

He pushes up on his elbows and looks down at me. "Your dad's a fucking cop?"

"Chill." I giggle. "It isn't like he would actually shoot you . . . at least not with the intention to kill."

"What?"

"I'm kidding," I say, and he lowers himself back down.

"So, he isn't a cop?"

"No, he is. That part is true. But I doubt he'd waste a bullet on you. You're harmless."

"You calling me a softy?"

Rolling my head to the side, I ask, "Are you?"

His only response is a smirk followed by a wink, to which I shake my head, but the slight movement makes the dark speckles reappear, forcing my eyes to pinch shut.

"You okay?"

"Uh-uh," I respond while keeping my lids closed.

"Is it your head?"

"My eyes."

"What's wrong with your eyes?"

Lifting my hundred pound hands, I give my lids a rub before opening them again, but the spots are still present.

"I had a bad head injury a few years back," I tell him without hesitation. I blame the pot.

"What happened?"

"My dad and I were surfing Backyards in Oahu while on a family vacation. He decided to call it, but I stayed out a while longer. It went from a playful head-high to a widow-making, triple-overhead in thirty minutes."

"Shit."

"I was trying to paddle out and around the entire point to get in when a steep wave with a thick lip came barreling down on me. The reefs are shallow in that area, and the force slammed me headfirst into the coral." My pulse kicks up from the memory. "I don't know how long I was unconscious or underwater, but my dad said it was a while before he could get out to me."

"That's crazy. So, what happened?"

"An ambulance rushed me to the hospital. I had a concussion and a skull fracture. I also had a lot of water in my lungs. I'm really lucky it wasn't worse, but ever since, I get these migraine spells and my vision gets really spotty."

"Is that what happened in the water today?"

I nod. "Yeah. I popped up on the board, and the spots became so bad I couldn't see anything."

"I had no idea," he says as he shifts to his side. "Does it happen a lot?"

"Last time was a few months ago when I was out with Brody."

Trent doesn't say anything, and the silence would be wracking my nerves if I weren't stoned, but then he sees the scar.

"Is that where you hit the reef?" he asks right before tracing the faint line with his thumb.

"Yeah. I was supposed to compete in my first competition a couple of months after the accident, but I bailed. A part of me wanted to take the sport on professionally."

"So, what's stopping you?"

"You sound like my dad."

"He wants you to compete?"

"Yeah," I say. "But that would require me to surf in the reefs sometimes. It's one thing to surf around here where it's nothing but sand. There is just no way I would ever be comfortable on a reef again."

He moves to lie on his back and tucks his arm behind his head. While he stares at the ceiling fan, I allow my eyes to fall shut. Everything begins to dissolve around me, and I surrender myself to the euphoria, finding it hard to hang on.

"You were right," I mumble so softly I'm surprised he hears me.

"About?"

Sinking deeper into the bed, I drift slightly before answering, "This is a much better high."

"You zoning out?"

"Yeah."

And right before I fade completely, I hear him murmur, "Me too."

Eight

"HOW HAVE YOUR MIDTERMS GONE SO FAR?" ADY ASKS.

"Ehh, fine, I guess." I dig my toes into the sand and tilt my face toward the sun.

"Are you ready to get algebra over with?"

"What do you mean?"

"Trent," she clarifies. "How bad has he been cheating off you?"

When she mentions his name, I scan the shore and find him down a ways talking to some girl.

"Surprisingly, he hasn't asked me for help at all. He actually has a better grade than I do."

Ady's brows raise. "Are you serious?"

"Yeah." I chuckle. "Honestly, I should be cheating off him."

"Maybe I should ask him for some help because I'm barely pulling a C in my Algebra class."

"So," I start, my curiosity elongating the word as I do, "why were you and Micah late getting here today?"

She rolls her eyes. "You never stop, do you?"

I laugh. "I just don't know what's keeping you from dating him."

"He isn't interested in me like that. Like I've been telling you, we're just really good friends."

"Uh-huh, right," I mutter, and she rocks into me, bumping my shoulder with hers. "How is it that you're so blind?"

"Me?" she stresses. "Oh, please. You're calling me blind?"

"What's that supposed to mean?"

"I see you sneaking glances at Trent. You still can't help yourself, can you?"

"That doesn't make me blind. I see him for exactly what he is," I say, motioning in his direction as he types his number into the bunny's cell phone, "which is exactly why I've never hooked up with him."

"But you want to," she states matter-of-factly.

"Not anymore," I lie. "He spreads himself around too much. It's disgusting." That part is the truth, though. I hate that he's been with so many girls, even girls I know like Jenna. Unfortunately, because of him, she doesn't talk to me anymore—not that we were ever close, but it's still annoying.

"You getting back in?" Brody hollers as he walks out of the water and up to me and Ady.

"Yeah, in a little while."

When he drops his board, he looks past the two of us, saying, "Yo, Van, what's up?"

I glance over my shoulder to see who he's talking to and spot two guys I don't know walking our way with boards under their arms. He claps hands with the one, who I presume is Van, and asks, "Where the hell have you been, man?"

"Just been working at the shop."

Brody turns to me. "Kate, this is an old buddy of mine, Van. He owns a surf shop right outside of South Beach."

He holds his hand out, and I shake it, telling him, "That's cool. It's nice to meet you."

He returns the sentiment before glancing at the guy to his side. "My bad. This is Caleb. He came into the shop last week asking for lessons."

My eyes go straight to Caleb's deep-cut abs.

"A newb?" Brody asks.

"Hopefully, not for long."

Caleb looks at me, and beneath this ungodly heat, a shiver crawls up my spine when he gives me a smile. I reach out my hand. "Hi. I'm Kate," I introduce, and when Ady clears her throat, I add, "Oh, and this is Ady."

"Hey, Ady." He nods to her before asking, "You two surf?"

"Kate does," Trent answers for me. I hadn't noticed that he rejoined us.

"Hey, I'm Caleb."

"Trent," he responds.

"Enough gabbing, time is money, my friend," Van says, and then he and Caleb head out into the water.

I bite my lip to hide my smile when Caleb gives me a quick look from over his shoulder before laying on his board and paddling out. Trent laughs when we all notice Caleb's rookie form.

"Dude, who's the nipplecake?"

Ady laughs, but I roll my eyes. "You were a beginner at one point too."

"Yeah, when I was, like, eight."

"You working on your tan?" Micah shouts at Trent from the water.

Trent grabs his board. "You coming out?"

"In a bit," I tell him. I watch as he jogs off and mutter, "His ego is annoying."

Ady drops her sunglasses over her eyes and smirks. "I don't think that was his ego talking."

"You're delusional," I tell her, reading between the lines of her statement.

We go back to watching the guys. It's apparent that Caleb is a total newb, but he's hot, so that makes up for all his embarrassing flubs. After a while, I grab my board and join the guys while Ady lies out and bakes under the sun.

I keep my distance from Caleb as Van teaches him the basics. It only takes him about an hour to tire out and swim back in.

"Poor guy can't hang," Trent says, and I shake my head.

"Hey, isn't that your bunny over there?" I tease, pointing to the chick he was hitting on earlier who's now posing on her knees like some wannabe model while her friend takes pictures.

He and Micah laugh and high-five each other.

"Don't be a hater, Kate," he says.

I maneuver on to my belly, and before I start paddling in, I say, "She probably reeks of Bath and Body Works. Girls use that shit to cover the smell of desperation."

As I dig my hands into the water, I hear Micah busting up.

"I can tell you haven't gotten laid in a while," Trent calls out. "You're becoming crotchetier by the day."

I flip him the middle finger.

When I drop my board next to my bag, Ady doesn't even flinch.

"Hey?"

"I'm trying to sleep," she garbles.

I glance over to Caleb, who is sitting off by himself, and he gives me an inviting nod to come over to him.

"Was this your first day on a board?" I ask when I'm close enough for him to hear me without my having to shout.

"Did I look that bad?"

I smile and sit next to him. "Not too bad."

"Even for a Midwestern guy?"

"Everyone has to start somewhere."

"And, it's actually my second day on the board."

I nod before asking, "So, where in the Midwest are you from?"

"Chicago," he says.

"You go to UM?"

He nods. "Junior. You?"

"Freshman."

"You from around here?"

"West Palm Beach."

His lips break into a smile. "That explains it."

"Explains what?"

"Why you look so good out there," he responds, tilting his head toward the water.

My cheeks flush, and I smile as I take in his well-defined jaw, which is covered in stubble and has me wondering what his style is when he isn't at the beach.

"How long have you been surfing?" he asks.

"My whole life."

"Well, it's a lot cooler than golfing."

"Golf?" I question. "That sounds like such a boring sport, if you can even call it that."

"Ouch!" he jokes, causing me to laugh.

"Don't you have to break a sweat for it to be considered a sport?"

"I do break a sweat playing golf."

"That's because you're just standing around in the sun. I mean, like an actual sweat from exertion," I tease, still laughing.

"You're a hard girl to impress."

I hang onto my smile for longer than I should before I force it away and sink my toes into the warm sand. "You're trying to impress me?"

"Apparently, I'm failing."

A hint of an awkward laugh slips out of me as I pretend to fuss over the sand that's sticking to my legs. "I wouldn't necessarily say you're failing," I timidly admit.

"So, would it be too forward to ask for your number? That is, if you aren't seeing anyone."

"No."

"No?" he questions, and I realize the misunderstanding.

"I mean, no, I'm not seeing anyone."

His smile grows, and, bashfully, mine does too.

Nine

KATE

I͟t͟'͟s͟ ͟b͟e͟e͟n͟ ͟t͟w͟o͟ ͟d͟a͟y͟s͟ ͟s͟i͟n͟c͟e͟ Caleb a͟n͟d͟ I e͟x͟c͟h͟a͟n͟g͟e͟d͟ ͟n͟u͟m͟b͟e͟r͟s͟ ͟a͟n͟d͟ ͟h͟e͟ has yet to call or text. I could just as easily reach out to him, but nerves keep me from doing so.

While I shovel a spoonful of cereal into my mouth, I consider sucking it up and shooting him a message. As I chew, a text lights up my phone, and excitement plasters a smile on my face, but I lose it when I see the text isn't from Caleb.

> Trent: Impromptu party at the condo tonight. Your ass better be there.
> Me: What's the occasion?
> Trent: Do we need one?

I'm distracted by my phone when I hear the lock on the door click, and when Piper walks in, I give her a suspicious grin.

"Where have you been all night?"

She tosses her purse next to me on the bar and grabs the box of Fruit Loops before shoving her hand into it and pulling out a fistful. "I spent the night at the sorority house."

She's constantly at the sorority house and sleeps there several nights a week. I miss having her around, but I haven't said anything because I know she's having fun with her new friends, and the last thing I want to be is a drag. It's just that I wish we could hang out more like we used to.

"There's a party tonight that I'm going to. You should totally come with." I really want her to say she will, but she hesitates just long enough for me to know she won't.

"I wish I could, but I already have plans with the girls."

It's the same excuse as always.

"I have to hop in the shower," she says before she scoops out another handful of cereal. "My last midterm is in a couple of hours."

When the door to her bedroom closes. I pick up my cell.

Me: I'll be there.

I also have my last midterm in a few hours, so after I gulp down the sugary milk from my bowl, I lock myself away in my room and, while I'm reviewing my notes, I hear Piper as she leaves.

I spend the next hour studying alone in my room, but grow tired after a while and give up. When Trent texts me again, I feel like he's reading my mind.

Trent: Just finished my last exam. You free for lunch?

Still full from breakfast, I go ahead and jump on his invite because I'm getting restless.

Me: Yeah. Where at?
Trent: Joe's Old School?
Me: Perfect.

When I arrive at the pizza joint, Trent is already sitting at a table. He gives me a smile as I walk over.

"I already ordered," he says. "I hope you like mushrooms."

"Gross. No. Why didn't you wait for me?"

"Dude, I have been, but I'm starving."

Knowing that I didn't waste any time leaving my condo, I eye him and ask, "When did you get here?"

"About five minutes ago."

"Are you serious?" I huff. "Five minutes?"

He smirks, and I know he did that just to get a reaction out of me.

"Whatever. I'll just pick them off." The waiter stops by and drops off the soda Trent also took the liberty of ordering for me. It's diet. I hate diet. But I don't give him the satisfaction of calling him out as I take a sip and pretend that it doesn't taste like straight armpit. "So, what's up with the party tonight?"

"Just a last-minute get together."

"Get together?"

"I've yet to christen the condo with a proper party. It's long overdue."

"Whatever you say. So, how did your exam go today?"

Our waiter returns with a huge pizza, piled high with veggies that she sets in the center of the table.

Trent is quick to grab a slice and take a bite. "Shit's good," he says with a mouthful of food, and I laugh at his lack of manners.

"The exam?" I question again as I start digging my fingers into the gooey cheese and plucking the mushrooms off my own slice.

"All I have to say is that I'm ready to be done with this macroeconomics crap."

"What about micro? Will you have to take that too?"

"I fucking hope not." He reaches for my pile of mushrooms, grabs a few, and drops them in his mouth. "What about you?"

"Yeah, I have to take it. It's required for my major."

"I still have no clue what I'm doing."

"I wouldn't worry about it. You'll figure it out."

He's unconvinced as he shrugs.

"Are you in a rush?" I ask before picking up my now muti-lated slice and taking a bite.

"Feels like I should be. Everyone around me is already declared."

"Well, what are you good at? What classes do you enjoy?"

"Nope."

"Nope?"

He takes a gulp of his soda, shaking his head at me as he does. He's flustered, and I find it endearing to finally see a crack of insecurity from him when he's always so cocky.

"Just say it."

He crunches down on a piece of ice. "You'll make fun of me."

"Probably, but I still want to know."

"It's nerdy."

"Doubtful. I don't think there's a single person that could peg you as a nerd," I tell him. "Come on, I won't tell anyone . . . promise."

He hesitates while he rolls his straw wrapper between his fingers, his eyes staying focused on the tiny ball when he reveals, "I kind of geek out when it comes to math."

"You're right," I tell him teasingly. "That's incredibly nerdy."

He flicks the paper wad at me.

"I'm kidding. I mean, if it comes easily to you and you like it, there's a lot you can do with that."

Again, another unconvincing shrug.

"Have you even seriously looked into the different majors?"

"Not really."

"Maybe you should do that this summer, you know, between your busy bunny chasing schedule."

"It's a time-consuming job, man, but I'll try and squeeze it in," he jokes. "What about you? You got anything good going down this summer?"

"Not really."

"You going home?"

"No, I'll be staying in Miami."

"Me too," he says.

"You aren't going back to Tampa?"

"No, I will, but for the most part I'll be here, so I guess you're stuck with me."

I smile. "I guess so."

When my time runs out and I have to get up to campus for my midterm, I tell him I'll see him later and head out. As I make my way up to the university, I call Ady to let her know I'll be at the condo tonight, but it goes straight to voice mail, which doesn't really surprise me. There are times she goes off the grid anywhere from a day to several; it's something I've kind of gotten used to.

My exam goes well, and around ten, I make the short drive over to Trent's. When the elevator doors slide open on his floor, the hall echoes with the thumping music coming from the other side of his door.

The place is already packed, and everyone is drinking. I quickly spot Brody from across the room, but before I can make my way over to him, Trent jumps in front of me.

"You made it."

"Who are all these people?" I shout over the music.

He leans in close to my ear, saying, "Fuck if I know." I laugh, and he hands me his cup full of beer. "Here, you're behind."

I raise the drink in appreciation before chugging a few gulps.

No need to take it slow and warm up when the party is in full-effect and Trent is clearly already drunk.

He slings his arm around my shoulders and leads me through the crowd where I run into Kylie.

She squeals and gives me a hug. "I didn't know you were coming," she says, tapping her cup against mine.

While she takes a long drink, I ask Trent. "Is Ady here?"

"Nah, I haven't seen her or Micah all night," he tells me. "Give me a sec, okay. I need to grab another drink."

Trent starts shoving his way through the crowd of people, and I turn my attention back to Kylie.

"I was meaning to call you today," she says.

"What for?"

"Jenna and I are going to check out this new hot yoga studio that just opened. There's an evening class next Tuesday we're going to go to. You should totally come with."

Clearly, Jenna hasn't mentioned anything to Kylie. "I'm not sure that's a good idea."

Kylie gives me a perplexed look. "Why?"

"She's pissed at me."

"What did you do?"

"Nothing," I tell her. "You remember that guy she hooked up with, the one you showed me the picture of?"

"Yeah."

I quickly scan the room and find Trent off with a crowd of people and point. "That's him; the guy I was just with. This is his place."

"So?"

"So, we're friends, and I think she assumes it's something more," I explain. "The three of us have a class together, and Trent and I sit next to each other. I tried telling her that nothing was going on with us, but she doesn't talk to me anymore."

"Wow, I had no idea. She's never said anything."

"Kate," Brody calls out as he walks over to me, cutting off my conversation with Kylie. "Refill?" He has a drink in each of his hands, and when I hold mine up, he dumps the beer from one of the cups into my empty one.

"When did you get here?"

"A while ago," I tell him before downing the alcohol.

When I hold my cup back up for more, he laughs. "Here, just take it," he says as he slips the half-full cup down into my, once again, empty one.

He then grabs my hand, and I tell Kylie, "I'll talk to you later," before he gives me a spin and we start dancing. Talk is short and benign as we bounce around to the beat. One song bleeds into another, which takes over another. Someone passes Brody another beer, which I happily pluck out of his hand.

"Greedy," he jokes as I take a sip and then give it back to him.

Tossing my hands into the air, I do a little turn and then spot Ady walking in.

Excitedly, I call her name, and when she sees me, she heads my direction. "Where have you been?"

I don't even let her answer when I grab her hand and pull her through the people to get her a drink.

"Look who decided to show up," Trent hollers, holding out a cup for her.

"I'm good," she declines.

"You in recovery now?" he teases and then turns to me. "I should tell you about the night I got this girl drunk for the first time. It was hysterical."

I laugh, take the cup from Trent, and shove it into her hand. "Come on. You totally need to have some fun."

Her reaction isn't what I expect as she stares into the cup and locks up. "I'll be right back," she mumbles before she makes an abrupt beeline to the back of the condo.

"Ady," I call out, but she's pushed herself too deep into the horde of people.

Not a second later, Micah goes chasing after her.

"What's going on?" I ask Trent.

"Who knows? The two of them have some weird thing going on," he says and then grabs my hand. "Come with me."

Trailing behind him, I let him lead me to his room, closing the door behind us.

"I got something I want you to try."

He pulls open the drawer to his nightstand and starts cracking up when he stumbles over his own feet, which causes me to laugh too.

"How much have you had to drink?"

"Enough to where I can barely feel my fucking legs." He laughs as he walks back over to me with a joint. "I picked this up from the dispensary earlier today."

I snicker when he holds it out for me. "What is this hippy shit?"

"Who're you calling a hippy?"

"You," I tease. "Who the hell smokes joints?"

"Oh, you think you're funny? I didn't know you Palm Beach girls were so posh about your dope."

I snatch it out of his fingers and correct, "*West* Palm Beach."

"Same thing."

"Completely different."

"Whatever," he mumbles as he flicks the top of the lighter and brings the flame to life.

I slip the joint into the fire before tucking it between my lips and inhaling. I don't even get a decent pull before the burning flower incinerates my throat and I begin hacking.

"Dude!"

Trent busts out in a fit of laughter as I choke, and when my coughing subsides, I smack his arm. "Like I told you before, I only vape or do edibles. I don't smoke."

"Try again, but pull a little weaker than how you would with a pen."

He watches with a lopsided grin as I take a hit. While I'm holding it in, he steps closer and takes the joint from me. From one unidentifiable second to another, my brain turns to mush, and I shuffle my feet until I'm backed against the wall.

"Good shit, right?"

I nod and exhale, already stoned as I watch Trent take a hit. Everything outside the two of us swims out of focus in complete disillusion.

"Don't waste this," he says when he leans in closer and braces his hands on the wall that's keeping me propped up.

He then opens his mouth and blows the smoke so close to my mouth that I'm able to get a second hit, but he doesn't even give me a chance to finish inhaling before his lips touch mine.

Immediately, I grab on to his arms before my knees give way and kiss him back, because, *oh my god*, Trent is actually kissing me. I can't even wrap my head around what the hell is happening when some dick bursts into the room. The kiss is over and done before I can even open my eyes—over before it even really began.

"You got some chick asking for you," the guy says.

"Here." Trent hands me the joint as if he didn't just kiss me. "I'll catch up with you later, okay?"

I stand here dumbfounded, trying to figure out if that really even happened or if I'm just so baked that I hallucinated it.

He stops short of the door and turns back to me. "Don't smoke all that shit. Save some for me."

He closes the door behind himself, and I manage to push off the wall and make it to his bed to sit, all the while trying to figure out what the hell just happened.

I catch a whiff of the pot, lick my thumb and finger, and extinguish the joint. After setting it on his nightstand, I begin to feel a pressure inside my chest. I thought Trent was an easy person to read, but that kiss has me questioning everything.

Was it intentional or was he just so drunk that he swayed a bit too close to me?

Did he mean to do it?

As soon as I ask myself, I already know the answer.

No.

If he had, he wouldn't be out there talking to another girl.

Stoned and way too vulnerable, I feel foolish. I should not be sitting here mooning over something that was an accident.

Pathetic.

The sounds of everyone having a great time echo through the door, yet here I am—alone. Aside from Brody, I'm not sure I have any real friends out there. Sure, Trent and I hang out casually, but so far, we've kept conversations pretty surface. And it isn't like Ady and Micah aren't cool, but I wouldn't exactly put them on the close confidant list either.

High and alone, I flop back onto the bed, ignore the scent of Trent that clings to the sheets, and close my eyes, trying not to think about anything at all and failing. When my phone vibrates in my back pocket, I'm offered the distraction I need.

Caleb: Hey, sorry it's taken me a few days to text. Midterms were no joke this semester.

And just like that, my smile returns.

Me: How do you think you did?

Caleb: I think I did all right? How about you?

Staring at my phone, I find it hard to gather my words, so I simply repeat his, hoping I don't sound like a weirdo.

Me: I think I did all right too.
Caleb: So, what are you up to tonight?
Me: I'm at a party.
Caleb: You want to just text me another time?
Me: No, it's fine. I'm about to bail anyway.
Caleb: That bad?
Me: I'm just not into it tonight.

And that's the truth. I mean, I was totally having fun until Trent kissed me two seconds before dipping out for some other girl. Now, I'm high and in a shit mood, which is the worst combination. The only reason I haven't left yet is because I need this buzz to fade before I get into my car.

Caleb: I hear you. I ditched out on hanging with my friends. This week has drained me.
Me: So what are you doing?
Caleb: I hit the gym and now I'm eating ramen and watching crap TV.

Ramen sounds good right now.
That bud is already giving me the munchies.

Me: Doesn't eating ramen completely defeat the purpose of going to the gym.
Caleb: LOL! True. I'm just trying to keep the balance.
Me: Ha ha! I guess.

The two of us continue to text back and forth, and when my high starts to wane, I sit up and stare at the wall where Trent

kissed me. The longer I look at it, the more pungent my sour mood about him turns. I'm over this party. Honestly, I'd have more fun at home in my pajamas, texting Caleb.

Me: Hey, I'm going to head back to my place. You mind if I text you later?
Caleb: Sounds good. Drive safe.

The music overpowers my head as I walk back into the living room. As I approach the door to the condo, I catch sight of Trent and stop in my tracks. He is in the kitchen, and the girl from the beach a couple of days ago is sitting on the island in front of him. Trent is standing between her legs with his tongue down her throat. It's a vile display that punches me right in the gut. What makes it worse is knowing that the bed I was just laying on is going to be the same bed he fucks that bunny on later tonight.

A mixture of disappointment, jealousy, and rage fire through my system, and I don't even know why I gave Trent the time of day as I slam the door behind me. Ady not only told me it was a bad idea but she also warned me about the type of guy he is, and even though I listened, I didn't *really* listen.

Maybe I'm better off resigning to just being friends with him.

As soon as I walk through the door of my condo, I head straight to my room, change into a pair of pajama shorts and a baggy T-shirt, and crawl into bed. Finally comfortable, I pull my vape pen from my nightstand, take a small hit, and text Caleb.

Me: So glad to be home. That party sucked.
Caleb: I'm glad it sucked.
Me: Why?
Caleb: Because now I get to talk to you.

Ten

KATE

"YOU'RE COMING, RIGHT?"

"I don't think so," I tell Ady while I stand in my closet and flip through my tops, trying to decide which one I should wear tonight.

"Oh, come on. It'll be fun."

"Fun?" When I land on my cute yellow silk cami, I pull the hanger off the rod and turn to show Ady. "What about this one?"

"I love it."

I toss the hanger aside and slip the cami on. "How do I look?"

"Perfect," she says as she sits on my bed and watches me get ready for my date tonight. "But seriously, you have to come."

"It would just be weird."

"Why?"

I walk over to my dresser and open my jewelry box.

"What's going on, Kate?"

After I slip in a pair of earrings, I turn back to Ady and admit, "Trent kissed me."

Her mouth drops. "What? When?"

"The night of the party at your place."

"Why didn't you tell me?"

"Because it was stupid." I walk over to the bed and sit next to her. "It isn't like it meant anything."

"What happened?"

"Nothing really. We got stoned, and he kissed me for a split second before one of his friends barged in the room. That was it."

"He didn't say anything?"

"No. He literally left me in his room to go talk to some girl who was asking for him, and when I sobered up enough to leave, the two of them were making out in the kitchen." Her eyes fall to pity. "Stop. It isn't a big deal. Plus, I'm over him." I stand and go in search of a pair of shoes.

"Great! Then you have no reason not to come to Key West with us."

I fall back on my heels and sigh. She's right. I'm not sure why I feel weird about seeing Trent again. It isn't as if I'm not totally into Caleb, because I am. Still, there's an awkwardness since I'm not even sure he's aware of what happened that night.

"Don't make me go with the two of them alone," she says, unrelenting in her quest to talk me into spending spring break with them.

"You say that like it's a bad thing when we both know it isn't. The three of you are best friends, you'll have plenty of fun without me tagging along." I finally find my pair of nude strappy heels and start fastening them on.

"You wouldn't be tagging along. I want you there because you're my friend . . . I don't have many of those."

When I look over at her, there's a sadness behind her words I relate to. It isn't easy finding solid girlfriends, and since the only other one I have is slipping away, I agree. "Okay, I'll go."

Her smile grows. "Thank you."

"It isn't like you're really giving me a choice with all your begging." I then step in front of the full-length mirror. "Do I look all right?"

"Yes. Stop fussing and go have fun."

As soon as she says it, there's a knock on the door.

The two of us head into the living room, and when I let Caleb in, he hands me an understated bouquet of flowers and smiles. "You clean up nicely."

"Thanks. So do you."

The one and only time that we've hung out together was at the beach, but seeing him now, I'm a little surprised. He's attractive, but his style is not what I expected. He is nothing like all the guys I hang out with. Where they are casual and chill in their appearances, Caleb is on the polished side with his dark-wash denim, trendy button-up, and perfectly styled hair. He's different from what I normally go for, but maybe that's a positive. It isn't as if I've had the best track record. Hell, I barely even have a track record at all.

"I should get going," Ady says as she grabs her keys.

"Oh, you remember Ady?"

"Yeah, it's good to see you again," Caleb says.

She gives him a smile. "You too." She opens the door, but before she slips out, she turns back to me with a flirty, "Call me later."

"Get out of here."

She laughs as she closes the door behind her.

"What was that all about?" Caleb asks as I walk over to the kitchen to set the flowers down.

"Oh nothing. She's just nosy, that's all." I find a pitcher for the flowers and fill it with water. "These are beautiful, by the way. Thank you."

"You're welcome. You ready?"

"Yeah."

He takes my hand and leads me down to where his expensive car is parked, and, like a gentleman, he opens the door for me. It feels good to have a guy know what it means to be respectful.

He takes me to Glass and Vine, and we sit on the patio under the palm trees, which are wrapped in tiny white lights. The evening is clear with the sky painted in midnight blue, and the music from an indie folk duo plays in the distance.

"This is nice," I remark.

"You seem surprised."

His facial features glow under the soft lights, as if inviting me to relax in his comfortable companionship.

"More like intrigued," I say as I pick up the stemmed glass filled with ice water.

"Intrigued about what?"

I take a sip and set the glass down. "About you."

He leans back and smiles. "What do you want to know?"

"What was your life like in Chicago?"

"Stressful," he states matter-of-factly.

I laugh lightly because how stressful can his life be at twenty? "How so?"

"My father is a portfolio manager at a large hedge fund. His job has afforded our family a comfortable lifestyle, but with that comes a lot of pressure."

"In what way?"

"In every way," he says, leaning forward and clasping his hands together. "I'm an only child to two very ambitious parents. I grew up with a nanny in a high-rise with a doorman and went to a prestigious private school. There wasn't any time to be a kid," he says before adding, "I was expected to hold myself in a way that caused me not to have very many friends."

"That had to be hard."

"It was."

"So, how did you wind up here in Miami? At a party school?"

"I needed to finally do something for me. To get out of Chicago and away from the constant pressure to be someone I don't want to be," he reveals. "It didn't come without consequences, though."

The waiter stops by, interrupting momentarily to take our order. I haven't had a chance to look over the menu, but Caleb goes ahead and orders a variety of small plates for the two of us to share, which catches me a little off guard.

"What makes you think I'll even like any of that?" I ask semi-teasingly.

"Because everything here is good."

I shake my head and laugh. "If you say so."

"Tell me about growing up in West Palm Beach. What was that like?"

"Simple, really. My dad is a police officer and my mom works in real estate. I have a little sister who is my complete opposite."

"How so?"

"Audrina can be dramatic whereas I'm pretty laid back. She's a social butterfly and cares too much what people think about her."

"And you don't care what people think about you?"

I shrug. "I am who I am," I tell him. "I spent most of my childhood with sand and salt in my hair. I lived in the water while she played with her dolls and tagged along with my mother to the spa for nail and hair treatments."

"Sounds like most girls I know."

"Not this girl."

"Are the two of you close?" he questions.

"We are; I'm close to my whole family, especially my dad."

"That sounds nice," he says in a way that's disheartening.

"Are you close with your parents?" I ask, already knowing the answer.

He shakes his head. "No."

"That's too bad."

"And my coming to Miami has put more strain on our relationship," he says. "They have much higher aspirations for where I should be attending college, and my trust fund continues to take major hits with each semester that passes that I don't change my mind and go back to Chicago."

"Does that bother you?"

"The money? Not really. It isn't as if it's going anywhere," he says, but I wonder if he truly means it. "To them, the only thing worse than having a son who doesn't care about his future would be having a son who is broke."

"Seriously?" I ask, shocked at their shallowness especially with their one and only child.

"Appearances are everything in their world."

"What about your world?"

"I guess I'm still trying to figure that one out."

Our server returns with enough plates to fill our table, but I find myself unable to peel my eyes away from Caleb. Sure, we've been talking a lot over these past two weeks, but our conversations have been far from the serious side of tonight's. Getting this glimpse into his life helps me to understand him better and connect to.

Even though I'm surrounded with people, most of them are surface relationships. Yes, I'm growing in my friendships with Ady and Trent, but those are still so new. What's been missing from my life since I moved here has been a solid foundation; a place where I feel I truly belong. With some friendships fading and others blooming, there's still something lacking in my life that's tough to explain, but with Caleb, even though he's new too, there's no bullshit with him. He makes me feel like I might not be so adrift. I know we only just met, but there's an authenticity within him that's comforting, something that has the potential to be deeper than what I have been able to find with anyone else here.

"So, tell me," he starts as he cuts into a crab cake, "what do you plan on doing after you graduate?"

"That seems a long way away."

"It isn't too long," he says. "Have you thought about it?"

I nod. "I want to work in PR."

"In what capacity?"

Unsure if he'll think my ambitions are trite, I go on and tell him anyway. "I really want to be a club promotor. Marketing and event planning have always been an interest of mine."

"Have you had any opportunities to get your feet wet yet?"

"The past two years, my mother put me in charge of her yearly banquet for her brokerage." I take a small bite of a crab cake. "Last year, I organized a casino night. I chartered the event on a luxury yacht, hired professional dealers, and designed the entire aesthetic."

His brows lift. "Wow, I'm impressed. And you took all that on while you were still in high school?"

"I had a little help, but for the most part, I did it on my own."

"That's amazing."

His praise makes me blush slightly, but enough for him to notice.

"No, I'm serious." He reaches across the table and takes my hand. "You really do amaze me. The more I get to know you, the more I want to know."

For him to see beyond my surface, to recognize that I'm not just a surf chick goes to show me that he's genuinely interested in who I am.

"What about you? Where do you see yourself after graduation?"

"Hopefully, still in Miami."

"You don't think you'll go back home?"

"It isn't what I want," he says. "Despite the fact that some of the top architecture firms in the country are located in Chicago, I'd like to stay here, forge my own path without it being handed to me because of the name I carry."

"Your family has that much influence?"

He nods before taking a drink.

It impresses me that, regardless of all the advantages he has, he wants to succeed on his own merit. That quality speaks highly of his character.

As we finish dinner, he glances to my plate and a tiny frown forms on his lips. "Was I too presumptuous in assuming what you'd like?"

"Not at all. The food was amazing."

It's hard to eat when he has my captivation filled to the brim. Talking to Caleb is easy to do because there's no beating around the bush. He's upfront and honest and engaging. It's refreshing.

After the waiter packs up our leftovers, Caleb drives back to my place and offers to walk me up. His manners reflect the upbringing he has described, which is something I'm not used to. Sure, my family has money, but we're so casual. We could've easily afforded to live on the other side of the bridge in Palm Beach, but my parents chose a more modest life for us.

When we step off the elevator, he walks me to my door, but I'm not ready to say good night yet. "You want to come in and hang out?"

"Are you sure?"

I bite my lip to hide my anticipation, but I fail, revealing an approving smile. "Yeah."

I close the door behind him and then head into the kitchen to put the food in the fridge.

"Is your roommate here?" he asks as he wanders into the living room.

"No, she practically lives at her sorority house at this point."

I turn on a couple of lamps, and the two of us take a seat on the couch. He's really close to me, and the butterflies multiply, causing my palms to sweat. Caleb shifts to face me, staring into my eyes with his hazel ones. My stomach is rankled with the best kind of unease. The kind you feel when you reach the peak of the rollercoaster right before the first drop. The kind that makes you feel each beat of your heart in every corner of your body. The kind you wish you could lose yourself in.

"I don't think I told you how perfect you look tonight."

His compliment sparks a flame that tingles through me, un-veiling an eagerness to kiss him. I'm not one to make the first move—maybe it's insecurity on my part, but I grow bashful, worried he can somehow read into my thoughts, and I become tongue-tied as I stare into his eyes.

He doesn't let my timidity linger for too long before he brushes his hand along my cheek and slips it back into my hair, pulling me closer to him. My eyes fall shut when I'm a breath away from his lips touching mine, and then he gives me exactly what I want—he kisses me. It's gentle, and I fall into it easily, kissing him back. A rush of elation stirs inside me, causing me to smile against his lips, and he feels it. He backs away, and when I open my eyes, he returns the smile, which offers me the comfort of knowing he feels the same way I do.

Eleven

TRENT

"KATE, MAKE YOURSELF USEFUL AND HELP ME OUT," I HOLLER from the living room. She and Ady have been wasting precious time gabbing while Ady finishes her packing.

"You can't handle it on your own?" Kate pokes when she emerges from Ady's bedroom.

"If you could've managed to pack your things in one bag, yeah, but you rolled up in here with all this shit," I say, staring at her two suitcases, duffle bag, and big-ass purse. "A swimsuit and towel is all you need."

She rolls her eyes. "Are you done?"

"Trent, be nice," Ady comments as she walks out of her room.

The three of us lug all the baggage down to my SUV while Micah finishes a phone call. Once everything is loaded and Micah is in the passenger seat, the girls hop into the back and we head south to Key West for the week. When I originally invited Kate, she gave me some lame excuse as to why she couldn't make it, but then Ady convinced her to come.

I haven't seen much of Kate lately. She hasn't been out surfing with us the past few times we've all gone, and when I texted to ask what was up, she told me that she was busy with school stuff. Apparently, school stuff is girl code for some dude she's started seeing.

"How did the date go?" Ady asks in a hushed voice, clearly trying to keep the conversation private.

Good luck.

When I glance into the rearview mirror, I find Kate with an obnoxious smile of her face. "I can't even begin to tell you how sweet he is—"

"Who?" I interrupt.

"No one."

"You mean Caleb?" I ask, and when she shoots me a snide look, I add, "That dude's a shubie."

"No he isn't," Kate refutes, but it falls way too short.

He's a total poser, coming to the beach in his name brand board shorts with his elite board, but the dude can barely hang a few seconds before getting axed by the waves he struggles to ride.

"He's a paddlepuss, Kate."

"You're such an ass, you know that?"

Her feistiness causes me to laugh. "Just calling it like I see it."

"So, because he isn't as good as you or Micah, that makes him a poser?"

"You said it!"

"Whoa," Micah says, piping in. "Trent's nowhere near as good as I am, so don't clump us together."

"Dick," I mutter with no hard feelings because it's the truth. Micah has managed to score a legit sponsorship and is taking the sport to the next level, which I'm entirely supportive of, but I bust his chops anyway. Can't let my boy get too big of an ego.

Everyone laughs as we fight the traffic.

"So, you let that dude take you on a date?" I ask. "Let me

guess, he took you to some cheesy putt-putt place and then out to eat at an equally weak place like Applebee's."

Ady laughs, but Kate quirks an irritated brow before saying, "I would imagine those are the types of dates *you* take girls on, but not Caleb. That guy actually has class."

"Fuck that! I don't take girls out on dates."

"Yeah, you just take them to bed," she mutters as if she's annoyed by that fact.

The thing is, I'm not the jerk she's making me out to be. Never have I bagged a girl without ever being one hundred percent up front about my intentions. So, if they get all bent out of shape afterward, expecting more, that's on them, not me. I'm not out to hurt people so I don't understand why her tone insinuates otherwise.

"So," Ady says, drawing Kate back in, "where did he take you?"

Kate gives me another glare through the mirror before telling Ady all about the dinner he took her to and their dwanky make out session on her couch.

"Can you believe this shit?" I say to Micah.

"Why does this kid bother you so much?"

"Are you serious, bruh? He's a kook."

"He is not a kook," Kate interjects.

"He looks like he belongs in a fucking boy band!"

"Oh my god." She sighs.

Micah busts out laughing this time, and Ady slaps his arm, saying, "You guys are so mean."

Micah throws his hands up. "I didn't say shit, that's all Trent."

"Pussy," I accuse. "You know I'm telling the truth."

"So, just because he isn't like you guys, you label him a kook?" Kate says.

"I just don't know what you see in him."

"He's polite," she says, holding a thumb up, and then she continues counting all the things she likes about him on her fingers. "He's smart, he's funny, he's hot—"

"I'm going to stop you right there."

"And he's an amazing kisser," she adds, holding up her fifth and final finger before flipping me off. She then turns to Ady and hammers her point in. "Like *amazing*, amazing."

"I think I might barp."

"Barp?" she questions.

"You know when you burp and a little barf comes up with it?"

"Gross," Ady whines through her laughter because, deep down, she gets me.

When we finally roll up to the hotel and check in, we head straight to the two-bedroom suite I booked for us. The girls squeal in excitement as they check the full kitchen, living room, and impressive view that overlooks the pool and white sandy beach.

They're quick to claim their room, leaving Micah and me to toss our bags in the second room. The four of us waste no time throwing on our suits and making our way down to the pool to bake under the blazing sun.

After a while, the girls bail to go shopping on Duval while Micah and I stay behind.

"Dude," he says as I'm just about to doze off. "What's up with you giving Kate shit about Caleb?"

"The guy gives off weird vibes."

Micah chuckles under his breath. "How so?"

"I don't know. You ever just get a sense about someone?"

"You met him for all of five seconds."

"Yeah, and in those five seconds he came off sketchy."

"You're full of shit, man."

Shaking my head, I reach over, grab my drink, and guzzle it.

"I think you've caught feelings," he says, and I nearly choke.

I push my sunglasses back on my head. "What the fuck are you talking about?"

"You're like the little kid on the playground who throws rocks at the cute girl because he doesn't know how to tell her that he likes her."

I crack up because he couldn't be more wrong. "Are you my therapist now?"

"Just trying to figure out why you're constantly stirring shit with her."

"I'm not throwing rocks. She's a down chick and we're friends. Period. And the shit stirring goes both ways, so you can suck my dick." I flick my sunglasses down over my eyes and lie back on the lounger.

"Pull out the tampon and chill."

"You're disturbing my Zen, dude," I say, and he finally fucking hears me loud and clear and stops pushing when there's nothing to even push.

About a half hour later, I drive the point home when I score some chick's number who's vacationing from UNC.

"Ady will kick your ass if you nail that girl in our hotel room."

"What are you guys, the boner barricade?"

⌒

Cranking the throttle, I fly across the water toward Kate, who's hanging idle on her jet ski. She's too focused with something on her life jacket to notice me as I close in on her. It's only when I bust out laughing that she looks up, and it's then when I take a sharp right and carve the ass of the jet ski in the water, sending a huge splash down on top of her.

"Asshole!" she hollers as I speed off, leaving her dripping wet.

I pass Ady, who's going in the opposite direction, and catch up with Micah. The four of us spend the afternoon riding on the water, jumping wakes, and having fun. Yesterday, we all went scuba diving. It was a long ass day, so we decided to just hang low at the beach today.

After we return the jet skis, we walk over to our spot in the sand, spread out our towels, and chill. I pop in my earbuds and throw on one of my playlists to drown out the girls as they talk. It's hot as hell, but there's a nice breeze kicking off the shore. Folding my arms under my head as I lie on my stomach, I'm halfway to fading out when the ringing of my phone cuts into the song that's currently playing. Peering over my sunglasses, I see it's my mom calling.

Not wanting to put our conversation on blast, I hop up and answer while keeping my earbuds in. "Hey, Mom. You didn't call to guilt trip me, did you?"

When I told her I wouldn't be coming home for spring break, I got the typical, "I can't believe you aren't going to come home to see me."

"I wish," she says, and I can tell she's crying.

"Is everything okay?" I walk up the beach and decide to head to the room so I can talk without so many people around. "What's going on?"

"Richard was served the divorce papers today while I was out running errands, and when I got home, he was here."

"What do you mean, he was there?"

Her voice rattles as she says, "When I walked in, he was sitting in the living room, waiting for me with the papers."

"What did he say?"

"He was really mad, and we fought," she tells me, her words shaking as they come out.

I use the keycard to unlock the door, and when I step inside the suite, I ask, "What happened? Are you okay?"

"I don't know. Everything escalated so quickly. I tried getting him to leave, but he refused." She speaks frantically. "He got in my face and was yelling. I didn't know what to do, so I called the police."

"Damn." I breathe heavily as I walk into my room and sit on the edge of the bed, feeling like a shit son for not going home this week. If I'd been there, things wouldn't have gotten so out of hand. "What did the cops do?"

"They just made him leave."

"Mom, you need to change the locks."

"I know, I just—"

"No excuses," I insist, growing upset at the mess this has turned into. "Garrett and I told you to do it weeks ago, but it still isn't done."

"I'm worried it's only going to make him more furious."

"It might, but at least he won't be in the house. You need to get the locks changed."

She takes a long pause. "What if I'm jumping the gun?"

"You aren't. This guy ripped you off!"

"But we're married," she stresses, as if that makes any difference.

"Mom, you dated him for what . . . six months before you guys decided to get married? I mean, how much do you even know about this dude?"

"I don't know," she cries desperately, and it kills my heart to hear her so distraught.

"You can't waver on this, Mom."

"I'm just scared. I'd never seen him like that. It has me questioning what he's capable of. I didn't think we'd wind up like this."

I love my mom, there's no question about it, but she's the type of woman who can't be alone. She jumps from one dysfunctional relationship to another. Growing up, our front door was nothing more than a turnstile of men coming in and out of our lives.

"This marriage didn't fail because of you. It failed because of him. You have to get the locks changed and change the alarm code too." I pull the buds out of my ears, toss them onto the nightstand, and switch her to speakerphone. "What did he say to you?"

"That he loves me and that there is no way in hell he will ever sign the papers. He said that if I moved forward with the divorce that he would make my life a living hell."

A bolt of anger shoots through me. "Have you told Garrett?"

"No."

It doesn't surprise me. I've always been the one she's turned to, the one she dumps all her baggage on. For years, I've been carrying the weight of her troubles on my back, even though I'm entirely ill-equipped to handle any of it. But I'm her son, and even though Garrett is older than I am, I've been my mother's main source of support since I was a little kid.

Leaning forward, I drop my head and fight the urge to start driving to Tampa. I hate that my mom is alone and dealing with this shit. There's only so much I can do, which makes me feel as if I'm letting her down. Deeper than that is the fear of Richard's erratic behavior and the possible danger it puts my mother in.

"Do you need me to come home?" I ask.

"No, I'll be fine. I don't want to ruin your trip; that isn't why I called. I just thought you should know."

"Look, we head back later this week. I don't mind driving over for a day or two."

"I feel bad."

"Don't. But just so you know, I'm going to call him."

"No, Trent. Don't get involved."

"Too late."

"Trent."

"Mom, he's threatening you, and you're sitting back giving him the freedom to do it," I berate, immediately feeling bad that I insinuated any of this was her fault because it isn't. "I'm sorry. I'm not blaming you. That isn't what I meant."

"I know," she mutters, and I can tell that she's crying again. "I never thought in a million years that I'd be in this situation with him. You should've seen how angry he was."

"Which is why I'm coming home."

"You really don't have—"

"I'll be there this weekend."

After a few more minutes, she promises to call about the locks and we hang up. To say I'm worried about her would be an understatement. I never expected Richard to act this way any more than she did. When my mother introduced Richard to my brother and me, I was surprised how easily he fit into our family. I thought this guy would be the lasting one. But they never last, which is why I refuse to commit myself to anyone, because, in the end, nothing ever lasts, and people always wind up getting hurt. I'm smart enough to avoid that rabbit hole filled with disaster.

When I step out of my room, I find Kate in the kitchen.

"What are you doing?" My words come out accusingly, which startles her.

"Grabbing drinks," she says timidly as she slowly places a couple of waters into her beach bag. "Is everything okay?"

"Yeah, why?" I ask, not wanting to talk about anything she might have overheard.

"Who were you on the phone with?"

"No one," I tell her. "Let's get back down to the beach."

She stares at me for a moment. "Why do you do that?"

"Do what?"

"Act as if nothing is wrong when clearly something is."

"I'm not like you," I condescend. "I don't need to go around *gabbing* about my problems."

She narrows her eyes at my tone. "I'm not asking you to go around and *gab*. I just thought, as a friend, you might want to unload whatever it is that's going on. And don't say that there's nothing going on because this isn't the first time I've heard you upset."

"I'm not upset." I'm annoyed. When I grab the beach bag for her, she pulls it away from me. "What the fuck?"

"Okay, maybe upset was the wrong word, but, clearly, you're angry."

"Yeah, with you." I drop my hand from the bag. "Are you always this nosy?"

"I'm not trying to be nosy. I'm just . . ."

Her words drop off, and even though I should leave them where they fall, I don't. For some reason, I pick them back up. "You're just what?"

She takes a moment before she responds. "I guess I'm just concerned about whatever it is you're dealing with."

It's strange to have someone meddling in my business. Sure, I have a large circle of friends, but those guys aren't the type to give a shit about personal drama. I don't get deep enough with anyone to even have to worry about that happening. Aside from my brother, Micah is the only person who knows about my family situation, and even at that, he only knows the bare minimum.

"Why won't you talk to me?" she questions as she walks around the counter to where I'm standing.

"I do talk to you."

"You know what I mean." She sits on the barstool that's next to me. "Can I ask you something?"

"Do I have a choice?"

She smiles and shakes her head. "Why do you keep people at a distance?"

I want to make a wisecrack to lighten the mood, but there's a sincerity in her eyes that's telling me not to blow her off with my bullshit. Kate isn't like most girls who tend to have an agenda behind their actions. She's a straight shooter, and since I'm stuck in this suite with her for the rest of the week, I don't need to be purposely pissing her off, so I give her a sliver of what she's asking and respond, "People can't disappoint you if you don't let them in."

"You can't shut people out without giving them a chance."

"Why not?"

"Because what's the point of having people in your life if you can't trust them?"

"Trusting people gives them an open invitation to fuck you over."

"Is that really what you think?"

I look her straight in the eyes and reveal, "My mother has been married five times, and all of them have turned to shit because she trusted too easily."

There's shock in her expression, which isn't surprising. Her parents are still married—she's one of the lucky ones.

"This shit is getting too deep," I eventually say, reaching over the counter and grabbing the bag. "Come on, let's go."

She grips my forearm and stops me. "Don't do that."

I could easily break her hold on me, but something tells me not to push.

She opened up to me about her surfing accident. She took something that she could've easily died from and handed it over to me effortlessly. All I had to do was ask, and she didn't even hesitate to tell me.

This situation with my mom has been going on for months. And while I'm good at compartmentalizing, lately, it's been consuming more and more of my energy. And now, finding out that fucker showed up at the house and scared my mother to the point she had to call the cops, I'm consumed with too many emotions to count.

I take the seat next to her, and she drops her hand from me.

"Who were you on the phone with?" she questions softly.

I fight against the urge to dodge this conversation, to avoid embarrassment, but I go ahead and admit, "My mom."

I'm not sure how to talk about this shit, especially with Kate, and it makes it hard to look her in the eyes.

"Is she okay?"

Instinct tells me to say yes and to drop it, but instead, I find myself shaking my head. "Her marriage to my stepdad has gone to shit. He broke into her house today and threatened her."

"Oh my god." She breathes the words. "What happened?"

"She called the police and they got him out of there."

Her eyes fill with worry for my mom, a woman she doesn't even know, and I suddenly regret mentioning it at all. "Don't say anything to anyone, okay?"

"Of course not," she agrees.

"I don't need people knowing this shit."

"I won't say anything," she assures.

Revealing this small piece of my life to her pushes emotions to the surface. It's like ripping off a scab—at first, there's nothing but a layer of flesh, but it only takes a few seconds for the blood to rise, reminding you that the wound still exists.

"I have to take care of something," I tell her as I stand,

needing space from this conversation. I pick up the beach bag and hand it to her. "Go ahead and go. I'll be down in a few minutes."

"Are you sure?"

"Yeah. I'll be down in a bit."

She gives me a reluctant nod, and I head back to my room, closing the door behind me because I need a fucking moment to collect my thoughts. I pace over to the large window that overlooks the beach and brace my hands against the glass. Taking in a deep breath, I force myself to temper the ache in my chest because there's no sense in getting worked up over a situation that's out of my control.

The pressure weighing on my shoulders hurts, and I hang my head, hoping to alleviate some of it. Then the door behind me opens, and when I turn, Kate is already walking toward me. I want to tell her to get the fuck out, but she quickly wraps her arms around me. Before I even realize that I need the comfort she's offering, I'm hugging her back. And somehow, without a single word spoken, she's able to soothe some of my jagged edges.

KATE

RAIN PELTS AGAINST THE WINDOWS, EXTINGUISHING THE SILENCE IN the room while Ady and I pack our bags.

"I can't believe spring break is already over. I'm not ready to leave."

Ady laughs. "And you didn't even want to come."

"I know, but I'm so glad I did."

All in all, it's been an amazing trip, but I'm also excited to get back to Miami. After my date with Caleb, I hadn't heard from him, and Ady made me promise not to be the first one to reach out. Luckily, I didn't have to wait too long. He finally called me two nights ago. I wound up camping out on the couch so I wouldn't wake up Ady. We spent hours on the phone, never struggling once with conversation. We could've talked until the sun came up if I hadn't fallen asleep on him.

"You almost ready?" Micah asks when he peeks in our room.

I watch Ady's eyes shift when she gives him a nod, and when I look over at Micah, he seems equally as awkward.

"What's that all about?" I ask when he steps out of the room.

"What do you mean?"

I toss my bikini into my bag. "Did something happen between the two of you?"

"No."

Looking suspiciously at her, I add, "The two of you have been acting weird all morning."

"I'm just tired. It's been a long week."

I get the feeling there's something she isn't telling me, but I drop it and let it go—*for now.*

The weather managed to hold out on us all week, but today is cloaked in dark clouds and heavy rain as we make the three-and-a-half-hour drive back to Miami.

By the time we hit the Seven Mile Bridge, Ady is sound asleep next to me, Trent and Micah are in the front, talking about random stuff, and I sit with my head propped against the window, watching the raindrops skitter across the glass. Turning my head, I look between the three of them and feel a strong sense of gratitude that they've opened up their small circle to include me.

My phone chimes and briefly catches Trent's attention before he goes back to his conversation with Micah. I stifle a smile when I see Caleb's name.

Caleb: When are you heading back?
Me: In the car now, but we are stopping in Islamorada for lunch. We should be back around four o'clock.
Caleb: What do you have going on tomorrow?
Me: Aside from laundry and catching up on all the trash TV I've missed? Nothing.
Caleb: Will you let me sneak you away for lunch?

His text makes my heart triple beat, and I can't ignore how good it feels.

Me: I'd love that.

About an hour later, the skies clear as we hit Islamorada and stop at Mangrove Mike's for some much-needed diner food. We get our fill of greasy burgers and tater tots, and when I can no longer go on in my gluttony, I toss my napkin onto the table and lean back in the booth with a loud groan.

"I think my stomach might explode."

"Same," Trent says. "I need to walk around."

Micah and Ady are still eating when Trent gets up and goes outside. Through the window, I watch as he walks over to his SUV, leans against it, and pulls out his phone.

"I'm going to walk around too before we hit the road," I tell the both of them, but neither pays any attention to me as I slide from the booth.

The humidity from the earlier rain hangs thick in the air. Shoving my hands into my pockets, I slowly make my way over to Trent. When he notices me, he shoves his phone into his pocket.

"What are you doing?" he asks.

"Thought I would stretch my legs before getting back in the car."

"Are they almost done?" he asks about Ady and Micah.

"Yeah." Next to him, I lean against the side of his SUV.

"So what do you have going on this weekend?"

I peer up at him, hesitant to mention Caleb's name, and shrug. "Not much. What about you?"

He runs his hand through his hair, which is growing longer by the day. "I'm heading back to Tampa tomorrow."

"To check on your mom?"

He gives me a nod when he glances my way, making eye contact for a brief moment before looking away. He's a person who has difficulty opening up, so I appreciate the small pieces he's able to give. Honestly, after the short conversation we had the other day, I feel like I understand him better. Finally, I'm able to connect some of the dots as to why he is the way that he is and why he would choose to keep himself detached from people, especially relationships. His childhood must've felt completely unstable.

"Let's get out of here," Micah announces when he and Ady walk out of the diner, and Trent says nothing more before he turns and hops into the driver's seat.

When we arrive at their condo in Miami, Trent helps me move my bags from his SUV into the trunk of my car before I head back to my place. As I'm struggling to lug all my bags into the lobby of my building, I see Caleb inside. He rushes over to the doors and opens them for me.

"What are you doing here?" I practically squeal in excitement.

"I didn't want to wait until tomorrow to see you."

He pulls me into his arms, and a warmth of happiness envelops me. His presence alone ignites a feeling inside of me that I haven't felt before, and I find myself wanting more, but I'm cautious to show him that. I don't want to come off as too eager or desperate. He's just so different from all the other guys I know—kind, gentle, and so sweet to surprise me here today that I can't temper the smile on my lips.

When he loosens his hold, he leans in and kisses me. Even though it's soft, it sends a shiver up my spine. A small chuckle escapes him when he pulls away.

"What's so funny?"

"Watching you trying to drag in all these bags."

I laugh and jokingly slap his arm.

"Seriously," he says as he grabs two of my bags, "you were only gone for a week."

"I wanted to have options," I defend as we make our way

to the elevators and up to my floor. "I still can't believe you're here."

"Is it that surprising?"

For a girl like me who hasn't had much experience with dating, it is a big deal. Aside from the guy I dated in high school, there hasn't been anyone else. It reassures me, knowing that Caleb wants to see me just as much as I want to see him.

When we walk into the condo, I call out for Piper, but get no response.

When I peek into her room, Caleb asks, "Is she here?"

"No."

He then follows me into my room where we drop my luggage on the floor.

"It feels so good to be home." I practically moan as I fall back onto the mattress. "I missed being in my own bed."

Caleb closes the door, walks over to me, and teases, "I missed being in your bed too," as he lies down and slips his arm around me.

"You've never been in my bed," I respond with a smile, but he quickly kisses it away.

Relaxing into his hold, I lose myself in his touch and the taste of his lips. He causes my heart to race in ways it never has before. It's as if his touch alone is telling me that this is exactly where I'm supposed to be, even though I've only known him a few short weeks.

His fingers thread through my long hair, and when we finally drag our lips apart, he gives me a quiet, "I missed you."

Before I can respond, I hear the door to the condo as it shuts, and two seconds later, Piper opens the door to my room. When she sees I'm with a guy, she hesitates in surprise, stuttering, "Oh, I'm sorry. I wasn't even sure you were home."

Caleb and I quickly sit up. "No, you're fine," I say. "This is Caleb."

"Hey, I'm Piper. I'm sorry I barged in."

"No worries," he tells her.

"Can I . . . can I talk to you for a sec?"

"Yeah, sure." I turn to Caleb as I get off the bed. "I'll be right back."

I follow Piper into the living room, and when I notice her wringing her hands, I sense something is bothering her. "What's going on?"

"First off, who's the hottie in your bed?"

"A guy I just started seeing," I say before asking again, "So what's up? What do you need to talk about?"

Her expression drops.

"What is it?"

"I don't want you to be mad," she says.

"Why would I be mad?"

She takes a moment before telling me, "I'm moving out."

"What?" I exclaim in shock. "Why?"

"See, you're already mad."

"I'm not mad; I'm just confused. Where are you going?"

"I'm moving into the sorority house. I didn't want to say anything until I knew for sure that I'd be able to get a room."

This news is a sucker punch, a complete derailing of the plans we made when we moved here, and I'm not sure what to say, so I say nothing as I stare at her—dumbfounded.

"Are you mad?"

I look out the glass door that leads to the small balcony as her words sink in.

"You're totally mad," she continues.

"I'm not mad, I just don't get why you would want to move out."

"It's just that, I'm always at the house anyway, so it just makes sense for me to move in."

I nod because I don't know what else to do. "No, I get it." And I do. I understand why she would want to make this move, but it leaves me to live by myself, which I don't want.

"Are you sure?"

I fake a smile for her benefit, but nothing about this makes me happy. The fact is that I *am* mad. I'm also disappointed and sad. I had so many expectations when we came to Miami together, none of which have happened. I love Piper, but unfortunately, we've found ourselves going in opposite directions.

"When do you move?"

"I won't move until our lease is up this summer," she tells me.

I give another nod.

"Are you sure we're okay?"

When I look at her, I can see her concern, and a part of me doesn't want to make her feel any better about moving out because, selfishly, I'd rather her change her mind. Still, I try on a smile and assure, "Yeah, we're okay. I mean, I'm sad we won't be living together, but I'm not mad at you."

She breathes a sigh of relief and gives me a hug. "Thanks for understanding."

There's a weight in my stomach as I walk back into my room.

"Is everything okay?"

Sitting next to Caleb on the edge of the bed, I slack my shoulders and release a heavy breath.

He scoots in closer to me. "What did she say?"

"That she's moving out." I swallow hard as my emotions thicken. I wanted to come to college with my best friend and experience everything together. I don't want to live by myself, and I know that when she does move out, we are only going to grow further apart. It feels like I'm losing a piece of my home.

I fight against the burn behind my eyes because I don't want Caleb to know just how upset I am. Taking a deep breath, I hold it for a second before exhaling with a somber, "This sucks."

Thirteen

KATE

FINALS JUST ENDED AND THERE ARE ALREADY BOXES STACKED AROUND the condo. With each one Piper adds, I grow more and more depressed about having to move myself. I can't afford this unit on my own, and with no single bedroom vacancies left in this building, I have to start looking elsewhere for a place to live.

I even asked Ady if she wanted to move in—more like begged—but she's happy living with Trent and Micah. And even though Micah and Ady are officially a couple now, she still wanted to keep her room.

With my freshman year ending, along with all the plans I had with Piper, I've been a little lost. There is one thing I've been able to count on, and that's Caleb. We've been dating for a couple of months, and I couldn't be happier. He's the one constant that grounds me, and even though I'm sad about my whole living situation, knowing that I have his support makes everything a little easier.

A knock on the door, pulls me out of my thoughts, reminding me that tonight is not the night to dwell on sad things.

"Wow," Caleb says as he walks in. "You look amazing."

"Thanks."

With my hair styled in loose waves, I strap on a killer pair of heels to finish my outfit, and I'm ready to go and have a fun night. School is officially out for summer, and Brody is throwing a huge party at the house he rents with a few other guys. Caleb doesn't really know the people I hang out with, but he's becoming a special person in my life and I'm ready to start immersing him into mine even more. My main hesitation is Trent. He's made it clear through his constant insults that he isn't a fan of Caleb.

"You ready?"

"Yeah."

Together, we head down to Caleb's car. He's looking all sorts of hot tonight in his signature casual button-up and his hair gelled. He opens the door for me, and I slip into his sports car. A minute later, we are on our way.

It's just around ten o'clock when we show up, and the party is already in full swing with music thumping and enough alcohol to sink a ship. Hand in hand, we push our way through the crowded house and find Brody in the kitchen, pouring vodka into a plastic cup for some blonde.

"What's up, man," he says to Caleb, clapping hands with him. "Help yourself."

While Caleb grabs us drinks, I wander into the living room where a bunch of people are dancing and run into some friends. I'm not surprised when I spot Trent. We always wind up at the same parties, and tonight, he's in usual form—drunk and dancing with some random. He spots me and gives an acknowledging nod at the same time Caleb comes up from behind and hands me a cup.

"What is it?" I holler over the loud music.

"Vodka and orange juice."

I take a sip and the burn checks me. "Where's the orange juice? This is straight up vodka."

He laughs, takes a swig of his beer, and we start dancing. The room is elbows to elbows, but I don't care. I turn around, lean my back against Caleb, and let loose after the stress of finals. One song fades into another as I dance the night away and party with my friends.

When my cup runs dry, Caleb asks, "Want another?"

Teetering on the line of drunk and sloppy, I hand over my cup and tell him, "A little more orange juice this time."

He leans in and gives me a kiss before he navigates through the mass of people, but I lose track of him when someone grabs my waist and spins me around. Before I know it, I'm chest to chest with Trent. His hands are on my hips as he moves in sync with the music.

"What are you doing?"

"What the fuck does it look like? You've looked bored out of your mind all night."

"What are you talking about?"

"With Caleb," he says close to my ear so I can hear him. "I figured you could use some fun."

I shake my head as we continue to dance. "I don't know why you do that," I say. "You're always riding his ass. And, by the way, I've been having fun all night."

"You're full of shit if you expect me to believe that." He takes my hand and turns me around so my back is against his chest. He then lowers his lips to my ear. "This is the first time tonight I've seen you smile like this."

"You're drunk," I tease.

"Possibly," he responds, and we both laugh. "Doesn't change the fact that a kook is a kook."

Grabbing on to his wrists, I pull his hands off me and turn back around. "You can't do that anymore. You can't keep talking shit about him."

"Says who?"

"Says *me*." When he shoots me a snide look, I get defensive. "I'm serious, Trent. I love him."

I say the words, and we stop dancing as his whole expression drops. "You're fucking kidding me, right? The guy is a shubie."

"So what? Why do you even care?"

"Hey, babe," Caleb says from behind me. "Here."

I take the cup from him and swallow a big gulp, praying that Caleb didn't hear me say that because I haven't even told him yet.

"How's it going, Trent?" he says, reaching his hand out, and Trent reluctantly claps it.

"Just showing my girl a good time."

If looks could kill, Trent would be dead with the daggers I'm shooting his way, but he doesn't care. Instead, the corner of his mouth lifts in a smirk before he says, "Catch you later," and walks away.

"What the hell is his problem?" Caleb asks in irritation.

"Nothing. Just ignore him."

And with that, I let my annoyance with Trent go as I enjoy the rest of my night. Whatever Trent's issue is, it's on him. I'm done trying to dig through all his bullshit to get to the root of his distaste for my boyfriend. In the end, Trent's opinion bears no weight on my feelings toward Caleb.

Caleb doesn't let it go though. For the rest of the night, he makes it a point to let everyone know that we're together. Whether it's him having his arms draped over my shoulders, holding my hand, dancing with me, or kissing me, it's evident to everyone, especially Trent that I'm Caleb's girlfriend. Possessive? Yes, but I don't care.

After a while, Caleb catches me stifling a yawn, and he takes my hand and pulls me close to him.

"I'm getting sleepy," I tell him.

"You ready to go?"

"Yeah."

I say a few quick goodbyes before the two of us duck out and head back to my place.

"Did you have fun?"

Despite what Trent said, I actually did have a lot of fun. "I did."

"Good," he says, taking my hand in his.

With my head resting back, I close my eyes as he drives to the condo. When he offers to walk me up, I take it a step further and suggest, "Why don't you just stay the night?"

"Are you sure?"

I nod. We've been dating for a few months, but we've taken everything pretty slow. He isn't a man who pushes, and I really respect that about him because I'm not a girl who likes to take things too quickly.

As usual, Piper isn't around when we walk into the condo, which for the first time, I'm thankful for.

"You need anything to drink?" Caleb asks as I head straight to my room.

"Some water. I also washed a pair of your gym shorts that you left over here the other day. I'll set them on top of the dresser for you."

"Thanks."

Opening the drawer, I pull out his shorts and a pair of sleep shorts and an old T-shirt for myself before going to the bathroom to change. After tying up my hair, I open the door to find Caleb already in bed. I crawl in next to him, take a few sips from the glass of water sitting on the nightstand, and lie down, resting my head on his chest.

With no more blaring music, the quiet stillness reveals the

slight throbbing of a headache. "In the nightstand on your side, there's a bottle of Tylenol. Can you grab me a couple?"

"Sure. Are you okay?"

"My head hurts."

He reaches over and opens the drawer, but instead of grabbing the bottle of pills, he grabs my pen and turns back to me, asking, "What's this?"

"Cannabis."

"What?"

"Pot," I clarify when I see his confusion.

"Pot? Like, weed?"

I laugh. "Yeah. Are the pills not in there?"

"No, they are," he says, but he's too distracted with the pen. "So, wait, you smoke weed?"

I stare at him, wondering if he's trying to be funny or if he's for real, so I proceed with caution. "Yeah." I stretch out the word, and when he doesn't say anything, I ask, "You don't seriously have a problem with it, do you?"

"What? That my girlfriend smokes joints?"

I bust out laughing because he obviously has no clue what he's talking about.

"What's so funny?"

"That isn't a joint." I take the pen from his hand and set it on my nightstand since he clearly has an issue with it. "It isn't a big deal."

The look in his eyes holds nothing but judgment, and I hate the way it's making me feel as if there's something wrong with me, as if I'm some junkie, shooting smack into my veins.

"Why have you never told me?"

"Because it isn't a big deal. Everyone does it, but it isn't like I sit around and talk about it just like you don't sit around and talk about the fact that you drink alcohol."

"Are you really comparing the two?"

"No," I say, growing agitated with the way he's speaking to me. "Just let it go."

Leaning across him, I reach into the drawer and take the bottle of pills out. I pop two into my mouth and swallow them with the water as he watches.

"What?"

"I'm just a little disappointed, that's all," he says.

"Disappointed? Really? Okay, *Dad*."

He cocks his head. "You know what I mean."

With a slight shrug of annoyance, I'm honest when I say, "Not really. You're making it sound like I'm taking bumps of cocaine when it's just a little pot."

He sighs. "I'm not trying to make you feel bad. Like I said, I'm just surprised, that's all. I don't hang out with people who do this stuff. And my parents would kill me if I ever did anything like that."

"So . . . don't smoke. No one is holding you down or forcing you to."

"I don't think we're going to see eye to eye on this."

"I don't think so either."

"Come here," he says, and when he tucks me in close to him, I relax into his hold. "It isn't a problem."

"Are you sure?"

"Yeah, babe. I'm sure. I didn't mean to upset you."

His ability to let it go so easily is impressive. He could've made a bigger issue out of it, but he chose not to, and it reassures me that he's the type of guy I want in my life. That we can agree to disagree and it's okay.

When he turns the lamp off, he gathers me in his arms, and I press a kiss to his waiting lips. Tonight, I don't want to stop. Maybe it's the alcohol lingering in my bloodstream that has me needy for his affection, but if that's the case, I still know that I love him and there's no reason to continue taking this relationship at a tiptoed pace.

My hands begin to freely wander when I slip them beneath his shirt. His muscles flex against my palm, and the heat of his body drives my desire higher. My lips travel down his neck, and he flinches when I hit a ticklish spot. He quickly flips me onto my back, and I giggle as I look up into his eyes, which are just as hungry as mine.

He rips off his shirt, and I follow next. With passion in his veins, he moves a little faster than what I would like for our first time, but I let him lead. His lips are all over me, kissing along my breasts and down my stomach. My heart leaps when he hits my pants, but after he slides them down my legs, he stops touching me. Sitting up on his knees, he shoves his shorts down and pulls out his dick before taking my hand and wrapping it around him with a wanting fire in his eyes.

When I take him into my mouth, he lets go of a sexy groan. Holding my head in his hands, he isn't rough, but he moves me to his liking.

"Damn that feels amazing." He moans, spurring my desire for more.

When he pulls out of my mouth, he stares down at me, and my stomach trills because I love him so much. I want to tell him, but I hesitate since he's yet to say it to me. It feels a little weird to be doing this without expressing our I love yous, but I don't get too caught up in that when he shifts on to his back and asks if I have any condoms.

The mood is shot for a moment when I hop off the bed and go in search of an old box in my bathroom. Tossing it to him, I crawl back on to the bed and kiss him while he slips on the protection.

He takes my hand and pulls me on top of him, wanting me to take the lead, and being as horny as I am, I don't waver. When I'm straddled over him, I want the profound words he's yet to give me, but the moment he's inside of me, I tell myself that I don't need them. Because I don't—I know he cares about me. When I begin to roll my hips over him, I hang on to the thought and let it seep deeper into my heart.

His hands grip my hips, and he begins controlling my movements over him, urging me to go at a faster pace. Pretty soon, the sensations that begin rushing through my body snuff out every thought in my head, and when he flips me onto my back, I'm a goner. Closing my eyes, I lose myself with him entirely, moaning as he thrusts deeper, driving me higher.

I hold on to him tightly as my skin breaks out into a light sheen. Our panted breaths fill the room, and it doesn't take long for us to reach our peaks and crumble apart in utter pleasure. When all is said and done and he's holding me in his arms, I lay my head over his heartbeat, feeling settled and exactly where I'm supposed to be.

I have no idea how long I've been asleep when a buzzing stirs me awake. It takes a moment to gain my bearings, and when I do, I notice a glow coming from my nightstand. Before I can pick up my cell phone, the vibrations stop and I see I have two missed calls from Trent.

Caleb is sound asleep next to me, so I slip out of bed and quietly pad out of the room, closing the door softly behind me. Once I'm in the living room, I flick on a lamp, which momentarily blinds me. After I manage to blink the shadows away, I call Trent back.

"I've been trying to get ahold of you," he slurs.

"I'm sleeping," I whisper, trying not to wake up Caleb. "What's going on?"

"Why the fuck are you whispering?"

"Because you just woke me up," I tell him as if he doesn't know a normal person is sleeping at three forty-five in the morning. "What do you need? It's late."

"I need you to drive me home."

"Why?"

"Because I'm fucking wasted," he says so loudly that I have to pull the phone away from my ear.

"Have Brody drive you."

"He's blasted too. Come on."

"Dude, it's almost four in the morning. Just stay the night there."

"There is a reason," he mumbles drunkenly, causing me to laugh under my breath.

"A reason for what?"

"I'm not quite sure."

"You make no sense."

"Wait! There is a reason why I can't stay here, I just can't remember what it is, but trust me. There is a reason."

"Stop saying *there is a reason.*" I huff. "Just . . . stay put, and I'll come get you."

"Ahhh, I knew you wouldn't let me down," he says with a jolt of perkiness.

I decide not to wake Caleb since there's no doubt he would be upset about my leaving in the middle of the night to drive Trent home. Caleb has done a good job keeping his thoughts about Trent to a minimum, but the truth is, Caleb doesn't like Trent any more than Trent likes Caleb.

Quickly, I slip on a pair of flip-flops, grab my keys and purse, and head out. Both Brody and Trent live nearby, so hopefully this won't take long and I'll be back in bed before Caleb has a chance to notice I'm gone. The streets are empty as I drive back to the party, and when I pull to a stop in front of the house, I spot Trent slumped over on the front steps.

"Are you okay?" I ask, and when he lifts his head, I see the level he's at. He wasn't kidding when he said he was trashed.

Barely able to open his bloodshot eyes, he reaches out for me to help him stand, and when I do, he hangs a heavy arm over my shoulders to keep from falling. Having to support most of his weight has me winded by the time I get him to my car, but I make it. Still, the two of us stumble as I try to open the passenger door.

"Trent, you have to help me out," I pant.

"Back seat," is all he mumbles, and I shuffle us a few steps toward the rear of the car and open the door so he can crawl in.

"Why did you drink so much?" I ask, not expecting a response as I start the car and pull back on to the main road.

"There is a reason."

"Oh god. Not again. Just close your eyes and try not to throw up in my car. We'll be at your place in a couple of minutes."

He doesn't speak for the rest of the drive, and in less than five minutes, we arrive at his building.

I open the back door and nudge him hard enough to get him to lift his head. "You seriously have to pull your shit together because I can't be dragging you across the lobby and up to the fourteenth floor." He doesn't respond, and I slap his leg a few times. "Trent, I'm serious. You have to help me."

I pull on his arms, and he sits up. "I got it, I got it," he groans as he stumbles out of the car.

Somehow, I manage to get him inside, across the lobby, and into an elevator. He holds on to me, teetering on his feet a bit as we start to ascend.

"Damn," he mumbles. "Your legs look fucking sexy in those shorts."

"I'll let go of you," I threaten, half kidding and half serious because it's way too late and I'm way too tired for his antics.

He manages to shift so that he's standing in front of me. My breath kicks up a notch when he rests his forehead against mine to steady himself from swaying. The closeness makes me anxious. He lets go of a sigh that holds more than just exhaustion, and I force myself not to let my eyes drop to his lips.

"Kate," he whispers an inch away from my lips, and my neck flames.

I shouldn't be doing this.

I breathe in the fumes of alcohol, and slowly shake my head against his. This isn't supposed to happen. Not now. Not like this. The fluttering in my chest feels more like heart palpitations. His hand finds my cheek, and my eyes fall shut in anticipation and denial at the same moment we reach the fourteenth floor. The jolt of the elevator causes him to lose his balance. He is still drunkenly fumbling to regain it when the doors slide open, his hand reaches into open space, and he falls ass backward out into the hallway.

My chest constricts with the breath I was holding as I was waiting, wishing, hoping.

What the hell is wrong with me?

I stare at him lying on the floor, passed out, and step off the elevator and over his body. I try to jostle him awake, but he doesn't budge.

"Trent."

I shake him more, but all I get is incoherent garble.

"Unbelievable," I say as a storm of emotions wreak havoc on my conscience.

My perfect boyfriend is in my bed right now, and I was just about to kiss another guy—*willingly*. Trent, of all people. The man who fucks anything with a heartbeat. The man who doesn't have the emotional capability to take anything seriously. The man who gives me shit on a daily basis.

"I'm so done with this," I mutter as I bend over, scoop my arms under his shoulders, and drag his ass to his unit, huffing with every step. His head thunks against the carpeted floor when I drop him, and it's mildly satisfying—but only mildly.

It takes me having to knock several times before a half-asleep Micah yanks the door open.

"Here," I say, pissed off at this whole situation. "I got him home. He's your problem now."

"You're fucking kidding me," he complains as he looks down at Trent. "Thanks for getting him home."

"No problem."

Micah is still trying to drag him into their condo as I step back onto the elevator, and I make a promise to myself that I will never let Trent get that close to me again.

Fourteen

"ARE YOU NERVOUS?" ADY ASKS WHILE SHE SITS ON MY BED AND watches me pack.

"Um, yeah. I mean, who wouldn't be? I'm meeting his parents." I toss another pair of shoes into my suitcase. "But I'm excited to see Chicago. I've never been there before."

When Caleb brought up the idea, I was reluctant. It took a little time for me to agree, but I made it clear that I wanted to stay at a hotel.

"What has he told you about his family?" she asks.

I walk over to the bed as I fold one of my blouses. "His dad is some hedge fund manager."

"And his mom?"

"I don't know if she's ever had a career, to be honest, but she doesn't work." I shoot her a smirk. "She's living the dream being a *kept woman*."

Ady laughs. "I don't understand people like that."

"Me neither. I'd be bored out of my mind."

"Exactly."

I go to my closet in search of a nice dress. "From what he's told me, his childhood was nothing like mine."

"What are you talking about? You come from money, just like I do. Just like all of us."

117

Pulling out my burgundy shift dress, I hold it up, and Ady gives her approval before I add it to my suitcase. "Yeah, we come from money, but I get the feeling he comes from wealth. Like, luxury wealth."

Ady's smile turns devious in a playful way. "You scored a good one."

I roll my eyes. "Oh, please."

We both laugh.

"So, do you have any exciting plans this summer?"

She shrugs. "The only thing that's set in stone is that Micah and I will be going to Tampa for a bit, but that's all."

"I'm surprised you don't go home more often. I mean, have you even gone back since you've moved here?"

She gives me another shrug to avoid acknowledging how strange it is. But that's Ady.

"I'll take that as a no," I answer for her when she doesn't respond, and she is quick to change the subject.

"So, when are you officially out of here?"

"In two weeks," I tell her as I close my suitcase. "The movers come the day after I get back from Chicago."

"Are you excited?"

"No," I say bluntly.

Piper moved out earlier this week, and it's been weird ever since. I'm used to coming home and her not being here, but to have all of her belongings gone? I don't know . . . it makes everything feel so different.

I miss her. I miss her more than what I thought I would.

"Well, you're always welcome at the condo."

"I appreciate that."

She should know by now that it's an offer I'm not likely to take her up on. It's been over a month since Trent almost kissed me in the elevator, and that was the last time I was at their building.

When Ady asked me why I never came around anymore, I told her what Trent had done . . . or had almost done, that it crossed the line now that I'm in a relationship with Caleb. It upsets me that he continues to push the boundaries and toy with my emotions.

It isn't as if I haven't seen Trent, but I don't go out of my way to be around him. If we're out on the water or at a party, it's easy for me to avoid him. He has texted me a few times, asking what was up with me, but I brushed it off, telling him I was busy with finals.

There is no doubt in my mind that he doesn't remember anything that happened that night, but I do. I remember the embarrassment, the guilt, and the anger at not only myself but also him for having no respect for boundaries.

"We should get going," I tell her as I wheel my luggage out of the room.

Ady helps me load my bags into her trunk, and the drive to the airport is uneventful outside of the heinous Miami traffic. "I expect a phone call when you land so I know Caleb is there to meet you," Ady says, sliding her car into an open gap in the departure traffic and parking.

"If I don't call, I'll text. Promise."

I give her a hug, say goodbye, and go inside to check my luggage before heading to the gate.

Me: About to board the plane.
Caleb: Can't wait to see you. I'll be there waiting.

He's true to his word, looking handsome in a pair of tailored slacks and a casual button-up as he waits for me down at baggage claim. I'm in his arms so fast. I let my nerves about this trip get the better of me on the plane, so it feels amazing to have his soothing warmth around me, quelling my unease.

"I'm so happy you're here," he says before kissing me. "How was your flight?"

"Aside from the screaming baby across the aisle from me, fine," I respond lightly with a smile.

"We need to get you some noise-cancelling headphones."

"No joke."

After we gather my bags, he leads me out to a sleek car that's even flashier than the one he drives in Miami.

"Whose car is this?" I ask.

"It's my parents'," he says as he loads my suitcases.

"Nice."

He opens my door for me, and we are off to the hotel.

"My parents are excited to meet you."

I smile, but it's forced. "Me too." It isn't that I don't want to meet his parents. I do, because I love Caleb, but it's nerve-wracking. This is the first time I've ever done anything like this, and I worry they won't approve of me.

Caleb takes my hand in his. "Why are you fidgeting?"

"Am I?"

"Are you nervous?"

"Maybe a little." *More like a lot.*

"You have nothing to worry about." He laces his fingers though mine and gives me an encouraging smile.

There's a lot for me to be nervous about. He's told me about how he grew up and the unattainable expectations his father puts on him. I worry they will take one look at me and dismiss me as a beach bum who doesn't have lofty enough goals and decide I'm not good enough for their son.

"We're actually going to meet them for dinner tonight."

"Tonight?" I say as my eyes fly in his direction. "I thought we weren't seeing them until tomorrow?"

"That was the plan, but they ended up making reservations for this evening."

I was really looking forward to spending time with Caleb, just the two of us. "What kind of restaurant are we going to?"

"A nice one."

"How nice?" I ask suspiciously, and he smiles. "Caleb?"

"You'll love the food."

I smile at his coyness. "That tells me nothing."

He gives my hand another squeeze, and I spend the rest of the drive taking in the scenery of the city. He slows the car and pulls through the valet drive. One of the attendants opens my door, and as I step out of the car, the staff is already unloading the bags from the trunk.

"We'll have these delivered to your room right away, Mr. Bradford." I give him an inquisitive look, and he explains, "I checked in earlier today."

"I would've been fine at a Hampton Inn," I murmur as he leads me into the elegant LondonHouse.

He laughs and shakes his head as if the Hampton Inn is nonsense, not really understanding that this hotel only amplifies my anxiety. My parents have always been on the modest side with their money; it's something I've carried with me since I left home. Caleb has always been a little flashy, but now that I'm on his turf, the contrast between us is stark.

The lobby is opulent with its modern décor and glittering chandlers. The stately brass doors of the elevator slide open, and I hate the pit that forms in my stomach as we ascend up to the eighteenth floor. Caleb opens the door to the suite, and I know he's doing all this to make me comfortable, but it's all wrong.

"What do you think?" he asks as I walk around.

I paste on a smile. "It's amazing."

"Check out the view."

I go to the large windows to see we are right on the Chicago River. "You really didn't have to do all this."

His arms come around me, and he presses a kiss to my cheek. "It's no big deal."

It feels like it is. I'm a college kid who only just turned twenty last month. So, to have my boyfriend whisk me away to Chicago and book this amazing suite for two weeks is a little overwhelming.

"What do you want to do first?" he asks, and I turn around in his arms and give him a devious smile, which he returns.

He sweeps me off my feet, causing me to squeal with laughter before he drops me onto the bed and crawls on top of me. Slowly, he drags kisses over my clothes from my stomach up to my neck and then grazes his teeth along my earlobe. I shiver against the sensation before grabbing his face and pulling his lips down to mine. Eager, I start unbuttoning his shirt as he runs his hand up the inside of my thigh. He's mere inches away from where I want his hand to be when we're interrupted by a knock on the door.

"Tell them to go away," I mutter as he sits back on his heels.

"Bellhop," a man's voice announces from the hallway.

"It's your luggage, which I'm assuming you need?"

"Fine." I groan in frustration when he slides off the bed and starts re-buttoning his shirt.

Caleb lets the man inside with my luggage, and I peer into the living room, quickly righting myself and smoothing down my hair when the gentleman glances into the bedroom.

"Is there anything I can get for you, sir?"

"I think we're all set," Caleb responds, slipping the man a tip before showing him out.

We spend the rest of the afternoon in bed, never making it out to explore the city.

Evening falls, and we exchange the bed for the shower, leaving me fully satisfied, but equally drained. While Caleb changes into his suit, I do my hair and makeup in the bathroom. There's a prickling of anxiety in my belly as I get ready, knowing I'm about to meet his parents, and when Caleb walks in to fix his hair, he takes notice of my mood.

"You look tense, babe," he says, leaning against the sink so he's facing me.

Screwing on the wand to my mascara, I stare at myself in the mirror and blow a few loose strands of my hair away from my forehead.

"Tell me why you're stressing out over meeting my parents." He takes my hand and pulls me in front of him.

"This is new for me."

"What is?"

"This," I stress, motioning to the luxury bathroom we're standing in. "I don't eat at fancy French restaurants or stay in expensive hotels."

"You act like you don't come from money."

"I do, but it's . . . it's just different. Sure, there's money in the bank, but it isn't as if I'm tossing it around."

He tilts his head. "What about that purse you bought last week? The one you spent nearly a grand on?"

Rolling my head back, I let go of a defeated, "Okay, okay. But that's just a handbag."

"An expensive one," he teases.

"I know. I get it. I like purses and shoes, but it's *different*."

"You've said that. I'm just trying to understand."

Dropping my head, I take a second to think about how to phrase it so it makes sense. It's about more than this room or this trip or the stupid purse I spent way too much money on. "Okay," I start. "Yes, my parents have money, but they aren't wealthy. I'm scared your parents are going to take one look at me and decide I'm not good enough for you."

He sighs and takes my other hand. "Babe . . ."

"I know. It sounds totally insecure."

"You don't need to worry about what they think. I think you're amazing, and that's the only thing that should matter."

His reassurance does nothing for my apprehensions, but still, I say a quiet, "I know."

"Besides, it's just dinner," he adds. "You're getting worked up over nothing."

With a subtle nod, I agree, "You're right."

"I know I am," he jokes, which has me cracking a smile that he kisses away.

"I'm going to go call for the car."

"Okay." I silently wish for another hour—or ten—to prepare for this. The preverbal penny is wasted because minutes later, Caleb is holding my car door open and I'm sliding into the passenger seat.

It's a short drive to the Chicago Stock Exchange. We take the elevator up to the fortieth floor where his parents are waiting for us inside Everest, a world-renowned French restaurant. My heels tap on the marble floor that leads us into the elegant dining area that overlooks the city, which is glowing against the nighttime backdrop. There's a black baby grand piano that sits away from the panoramic windows where an elderly man is playing.

My palm sweats against Caleb's hand as the hostess leads us over to the table where his parents are sitting. The two of them look so polished. His father is handsome and clean cut with a full head of silver hair, and his mother is perfectly poised with a single strand of pearls around her neck. As we approach, his dad takes notice and stands, looking sharp in a three-piece suit. His mom looks up, and she gives me a beaming smile.

"Kate," she greets warmly. "Oh, it's so good to meet you."

She then pulls me in for a warm hug, calming my nerves just like that.

"It's nice to meet you too, Mrs. Bradford."

"Please, call me Rose."

I smile. How could anyone be scared of a woman named Rose?

"This is my father, Conrad," Caleb introduces.

"Nice to meet you," I say as he leans in to peck my cheek.

"Please, have a seat. I hope you don't mind, but I ordered degustation menu for all of us."

"Oh, thank you," I respond even though I have no clue what that even is.

The waiter stops by and Caleb orders wine for himself and an iced tea for me.

"Were you able to do any sightseeing today?" Rose asks. "Caleb told us this is your first time in Chicago."

"It is. I was so tired from traveling that we didn't get a chance to see the city." I take a sip of my water, blushing on the inside at the memory of having sex with her son all afternoon. "I think Caleb is taking me over to Millennium Park tomorrow."

"That sounds fun." She looks to Caleb. "You should take her to Wildberry for brunch." She turns back to me, adding, "They have the best Florence Benedict."

"I love eggs Benedict."

"She's here for two weeks, Mom. I'm sure we'll be able to hit all the spots."

His father takes a sip from his lowball, the ice rattling against the crystal. "So, Caleb tells me you're majoring in communications. Do you know what you'd like to do with that?"

"I'd really like to get into event planning or public relations."

"I studied English Literature in college," Rose says. "It's been a dream of mine to have something published."

"Wow. Caleb didn't tell me you're a writer."

She fingers the strand of pearls around her neck. "Well, an *aspiring* writer."

"She's been working on her novel since before Caleb was born." His dad says, and my eyes stall on him because I expected some kind of teasing mirth but only find lukewarm annoyance. As if his wife's dream is nothing but a nuisance.

"These things take time," she says to Conrad.

"What's it about?"

She smiles without a single wrinkle around her eyes— thanks to Botox, most likely. "It's a historical romance that un- folds in the English countryside during the seventeenth century."

"Sounds interesting."

"Don't get her started," Caleb says, shooting his mom a smile.

"So, tell me, how did the two of you meet?" she asks.

"On the beach. We were both out surfing one day."

"Surfing?" his father interjects with a slight sneer as he eyes Caleb.

"It's nothing serious," he explains. "Just something fun to do."

"Hmm."

"The true talent is Kate."

"Oh really?" his mother says.

"Well, I wouldn't go as far as to say true talent, but I grew up surfing. My dad taught me when I was little," I tell her. "It's always been our thing."

"Is all your family in Miami?"

I turn back to Conrad. "No, I'm from West Palm Beach."

"And what do your parents do?" It feels as if Conrad is inter- rogating me, and my palms start to sweat again.

I tell him about my mom and dad and try to read his

expression, but he's unreadable, which has my unease spiking even higher. Where Caleb's mom is warm and inviting, his father is stoic and intimidating. Caleb's hand finds my knee under the table and gives a gentle squeeze.

"Real estate," he notes about my mother. "What type?"

"Residential."

"Luxury residential," Caleb quickly corrects, and the fact that he felt like he had to clarify that bothers me. This is exactly what I feared would happen. One or both of his parents wouldn't approve of me, and I would be dismissed.

The waiter returns with our first course, and I couldn't be more grateful for the etiquette classes my mother enrolled me in as a child. Of course, I hated her at the time because I wanted to be at the beach and not in some stuffy banquet hall with thirty other girls. I don't hesitate before I pick up the proper fork to use for my lobster. I then trade the fork for a spoon and dip it into the corn soup that's accompanying the lobster, remembering to scoop away and never toward. At least I won't have to worry about his father secretly criticizing my manners.

"And your father is a cop. That's a very honorable career," he compliments, not having touched his own food yet. "Is he a detective?"

"No, he's a uniformed officer. In his younger years, he spent many years on the SWAT force and he also worked as a DEA. Now he's behind the wheel."

As I tell him this, he flicks his eyes over to Caleb with an expression I can clearly read—he's unimpressed. I really don't like that this man is judging the very parents I look up to and admire. They both work hard in different ways, and they love each other deeply.

My dad didn't come from money, but my mother did—a lot of money. The two of them met in college. She didn't care that he was taking out loans and busting his butt having to work between classes. She fell in love with him regardless. Every time my father tells me about how he and mom met, I can't help but smile.

"That sounds dangerous," Rose comments, dipping her spoon into her soup. She then looks to Caleb. "Have you met them?"

"Not yet, but I have talked to them over the phone."

"You're close?" she asks me.

I nod.

"That's so nice."

"Son, I spoke to Harrison Astor. You remember the Astors, don't you?"

"Yes."

"He and I met for lunch the other week, and he's interested in speaking with you about a possible position after you graduate."

"But they're exclusive to Chicago. They don't have any other offices, right?"

"Chicago's your home, Son."

"Yes, but—"

"We'll discuss it further another day," his father says, cutting him off.

There is tension in Caleb that wasn't there a few moments ago, so I brush my hand over his, which is still on my knee. Then I turn to Rose. "What do you recommend to be the must-do things while I'm here?"

She perks up, and thankfully, we are able to stay on this topic throughout the next several courses. As the night winds down and I can't eat another bite, I thank Caleb's parents for a wonderful dinner.

"It's our pleasure," Rose says as we make our way down

to the lobby. "I'm looking forward to having you over later this week for dinner.

"Is there anything I can help with?"

"There's no need for us to get our hands dirty. I've hired a chef to prepare all the food," she tells me as we step off the elevator and into the lobby. "You'll love Nigel's food. He's one of the most sought after in the city."

"Oh, wow." It's a bit over the top for my liking, but I give her a polite smile. "I'm looking forward to it."

After we say our goodbyes, Caleb and I head back to the hotel, and as soon as we walk into our suite, I plop down onto the sofa in the living room.

Caleb slips off his tie and unfastens the top button of his shirt. "See, that wasn't so bad."

The same smile I gave his mother finds its way back onto my lips. Sure, his mother was pleasant enough, but his dad . . . not so much. "Your father seems to want you back in Chicago," I remark as I kick off my heels.

"I'm happy in Miami, you know that."

"Does he?"

Caleb sits next to me and pulls my legs onto his lap. "I've told him, but he only hears what he wants to hear."

Fifteen

KATE

THIS PAST WEEK HAS BEEN AMAZING. CALEB HAS TAKEN ME ALL OVER the city, showing me around the Navy Pier, Millennium Park, and Michigan Avenue. We've eaten amazing food and went to see a Cubs game, where they snatched the win from the St. Louis Cardinals.

Yesterday was the best day yet. We took a trip over to Matthiessen State Park. Everything about that place was spectacular, from the Cascade Falls, where the canyon drops forty-five feet and the Lower Dell begins, to the mineral springs and salt licks.

When we got back, we were both too exhausted to eat. We woke up this morning, starving, and ended up ordering half the items on the room service menu. The smell of leftover waffles and maple syrup lingers in the air as we get ready to head over to his parents'. Caleb and his dad are going golfing, so I decided I would venture off by myself to do some shopping along The Magnificent Mile.

"You about ready?"

"Yep!" I respond, excited for the day to begin. "What time is dinner at your parents' tonight?"

"Seven thirty."

As we drive over to The Loop, I ask, "So what do you think your father wants to talk to you about?"

"More than likely, my plans for after graduation next year, which is why it's a good idea that you aren't around."

"Why?"

"Because I doubt the conversation is going to go well."

I reach across the center console and slip my hand over his. He's been tense all morning, and I can understand why. The limited time spent with Conrad earlier this week at dinner made me really want to avoid any other interaction with him. He was intense.

"This is it," he notes as we drive around the front of the building and into the private parking garage.

"*This* is where you grew up?"

"Yes."

There is no backyard to play in or neighbors' houses to hang out at. I live in a high-rise in Miami, but to grow up in one seems so unfortunate. Having summertime cookouts and roasting marshmallows in the fire pit are some of my favorite memories. Caleb wouldn't have experienced any of that.

I decide to follow him up and say a quick hello to his parents before I breakaway for the day. Nothing about the black marbled lobby feels homey. With its dim lighting and eerie quietness, it's more like a commercial property than a home.

"Good morning, Mr. Bradford," the uniformed guard greets from behind a massive desk.

"Hey, Bruno," Caleb responds as he leads me over to the bank of elevators, and once we've reached the fifty-third floor, he leads me into the home he grew up in.

The lavish condo, which is a stark contrast to the contemporary lobby, is outfitted in dark wood, gold accents, and heavy drapes. My lungs fill with the scent of leather as we walk through the foyer and into the main section of living space.

"Honey, is that you?" his mother calls out right before she

rounds the corner. She gives her son a hug before addressing me. "Welcome to our home. Come in, come in."

I smile as I follow her into the sitting room, which boasts a spectacular view over Millennium Park.

"Your home is beautiful."

"Thank you, dear," she says before motioning to the large chesterfield sofa. "Please, have a seat. Can I get you anything to drink? A cup of tea?"

"Yes, thank you."

"I thought you were going to be here an hour ago." His father strides into the room and walks right over to where I'm sitting, and I stand as he approaches and kisses my cheek. "Kate, welcome."

"Thank you. Your home is lovely."

He gives a curt nod before turning to Caleb. "Come back to my office. I have something I want to show you."

"I'll see you later?" Caleb says to me, giving me a hug goodbye.

"I'll text you later."

He gives me a sweeping kiss and then joins his father as they leave the room.

"Come into the kitchen," Rose offers. "Let's have that cup of tea before you head out."

The kitchen is as elaborate as the rest of the space, and I take a seat at the massive island while Rose starts heating a kettle of water.

"So, what are your plans for the day?"

"I figured I'd take it easy and do some shopping."

"It's a good day for that since you'll be without Caleb. He hates shopping."

I laugh because it's so true. "Tell me about it. I dragged him out to Bal Harbour so I could buy a handbag, and I swear I had to bribe him with ice cream to keep the complaining at bay."

She laughs as she pulls down the tea cups. "That sounds like Caleb. When he was little, it was like pulling teeth to take him shopping for clothes. One day, I gave up and handed the nanny my credit card and told her to take him."

I join in her laughter, but part of me doesn't find it all that funny. She just handed him off to the nanny to deal with?

She joins me at the island and gives me an endearing smile as she sets a teacup in front of me. "I have to say, I've never seen my son so . . . relaxed. He's normally walking around, brooding." She covers my hand with her own for a moment when she adds in a softer tone, "You bring out a side to him I don't get to see very often."

"That's really sweet of you to say."

"Tell me, how are you liking Chicago."

"I love it," I respond. "The vibe is . . . well, it's a lot different from Miami, that's for sure."

Her brows lift in agreeance as she takes a sip. "Do you see yourself there after you graduate?"

"I do. I mean, it's home for me. I like having my parents close by."

"I understand that. Family is my comfort. Now that Caleb is gone, it just isn't the same."

There's a lapse in our conversation, and as I take another look around, I soak in the cold lifelessness of this place and wonder if it had the same lack of warmth when Caleb was a little kid. It's difficult to imagine him running around here and playing with toys—it's too pristine. I doubt anyone has ever been comfortable enough to toss their shoes aside and kick their feet up onto the coffee table.

"Were there a lot of kids in this building when Caleb was growing up?" I ask out of curiosity.

"A few, but Caleb mostly kept to himself. He was a very quiet boy."

Her response sparks a sadness in me. Although I still find him more on the quiet, reserved side, I get the impression that as a child, it was more so. How could it not be? This home—this building—it feels isolating.

When I drink my last sip, I smile and slip out from my chair. "I should probably get going."

"Yes! I don't want to keep you."

"Thank you for the tea. I really enjoyed our visit." When she picks up the saucers, I ask, "Where's the restroom?"

She motions to the hallway across from the sitting room. "Right down there, third door to your left."

I wander down the hall, and when I pass a large set of double doors, I hear Caleb and his father talking inside the room beyond, but I don't linger. While in the restroom, I try to ignore Conrad's voice as it grows stern. But, by the time I'm rinsing the soap from my hands, I've abandoned any guise of pretense and am actively eavesdropping. I focus and try to hear what they're talking about but struggle to make out their words. Whatever they're discussing, it has them both angry.

After drying my hands, I slip out of the bathroom and quietly walk toward the office. There's a slight crack between the doors that's wide enough to peer through. The urge to spy causes an unease in my gut. I peek around the corner and find Rose busying herself in the kitchen. She's too far away to notice me or hear anything, so I duck back behind the wall and sneak a look through the crack. It isn't what I see that disturbs me, but the hostility in Conrad's voice. They stand on opposite sides of a large desk and his father throws his fist down against the wood, causing a loud *thunk* that startles me.

"What do you mean you aren't coming back?"

"I'm staying in Miami."

"To do what? Waste your time, slumming it with that girl you brought here?"

"Her name is Kate, and she's far from slum." Caleb defends me with a ferocity I've never heard from him before, but it does nothing to alleviate the boulder that's pressing on my stomach as I listen.

Conrad stalks over to Caleb and gets in his face as he seethes, "I won't allow you to disgrace this family. After graduation, playtime is over, and you *will* come back home."

"For what?"

"You have a name to uphold in this town," he shouts, and I jump at the boom of his voice.

A blaze of fear stabs me, and I cower back from the door and lean against the wall, all the while feeling sick over how he's talking to Caleb.

"With this family comes expectations."

"Which is why I'm happy in Miami."

"Failures aren't happy people, Son."

"It just kills you, doesn't it? The fact that you can't control me anymore."

There's a loud scuffle, and I leap over to the door and peer through the crack just in time to see Conrad strike Caleb with the back of his hand. My heart catapults, and I choke on my next breath.

My pulse races in terror as Caleb shouts, "Son of a bitch!"

"Get your ass back here!"

Slowly, I step away as panic loops around my lungs and the ricochet of my heart pounds violently in my chest. When the door flies open and slams against the wall, I jump in terror. Caleb's eyes are wide and venomous, and there's a gash on his cheekbone that's dripping blood.

I'm horror-stricken, staring at him before he snaps, "What the fuck are you still doing here?"

The acidity in his voice burns straight through me, and I bolt because I don't know what else to do. Fear drives my feet as I rush through the large space and fly out the door. I run to the elevators and begin stabbing my finger against the button over and over as if it will get me out of here faster if I press it enough times. When the doors slide open, I dash inside and smash my finger against the door close button. The moment I'm enclosed in the small space, I stumble back against the wall, my chest heaving in disbelief and fear.

I close my eyes, but all I see are Caleb's scathing ones staring back at me, causing my heart to pound from beneath my ribs. Rattled to the core, my hands tremble, and I don't even know how to process what I just saw. I swear there was poison in his voice when he spoke to me, a poison I never imagined him to be in possession of, but he is, and he just spit it right at me.

When the elevator dumps me off in the lobby, I force my legs to move, but my knees won't stop shaking as I find my way out to the parking garage and into Caleb's car. Leaning my head back, I stare up and take in a slow breath. My heart says I should be crying, but the fear running rampant through me overpowers it. There are too many emotions that cripple me from making sense of it all.

Never in my life has my mother or father ever spoken to me the way his father just spoke to him. I can't even fathom my parents treating me like that, degrading me—hitting me.

I consider going back because I love Caleb and I want to protect him, but I'm worried he's pissed at me. I wonder if he knows that I was sneaking around and spying on him?

I'm too scared to find out.

After seeing the look in his eyes—the way they sharpened

like a dagger, as if he wanted to hurt me with them, I'm not sure I want to go back.

A million thoughts have my head spiraling in every direction possible. I have no clue what to do in this situation.

Gripping the steering wheel, I drop my head and tell myself that I'm okay to leave. If Caleb wanted me there, he wouldn't have reacted the way he did. And if he's pissed because I saw something he never wanted me to see, I'm sure returning would only make things worse, and that's the last thing I want.

I go ahead and start the car, but when I pull out of the garage, I head over to the hotel instead of toward the stores. There's no way I could possibly enjoy a day of shopping after what just happened—I'm too frazzled.

For hours, I sit on the sofa and stare out the windows. My conscience pushes me to do something—call him, text him, go back and get him, but none of those options feel right to me.

Truth is, if I had him here, I wouldn't even know what to say.

As my anxiety begins to dissolve, I turn on the television and do my best to focus on something other than the monstrosity across town. When I lose interest in the show, I pace around the suite, wondering how much longer it will be until he calls me.

If he even calls me at all.

But if he does, what do I say?

Do I ask if he's all right? Do I not say anything at all and act as if nothing happened and wait to see if he brings it up?

My phone never rings.

As the day drags on, I grow antsy in the confinement of this room and decide a walk might do me some good. I stroll down the river and meander around, killing time. As boats float by and tourists snap pictures of the surroundings, a whole new slew of tension begins to compound. I have to go back there for dinner tonight.

Just the thought of it has me sick to my stomach. I want to call someone, anyone, and talk about what happened this morning, but who? There is no one I would even be comfortable sharing this with, and I'm positive Caleb wouldn't want anyone knowing.

I find a bench and take a seat. Staring blankly down the river, I go numb for a while as the city bustles around me. In the midst of all these people, I'm so alone with my only comfort back at the one place I never want to return to.

Time passes slowly, and the tension awakens a dull thumping from behind my eyes. It's weak at first, but eventually, the pulsating swells into sharp pains, and I know this is the onset of another migraine episode, which is the last thing I want to be dealing with today. The moment my vision goes splotchy, I head back to the hotel.

Once I'm in the suite, I take my prescription out of my suitcase, pop a pill, and lie in bed. I spend the rest of the day dozing and don't bother eating anything. It wouldn't stay down anyway. The sun is starting to set when I pull myself from the bed, but my anxiety hasn't waned. The plan was for me to drive back over there around seven, but how can I possibly do that now? How do I go over there and pretend as if nothing happened?

I reach for my phone to see how much time I have left before I have to leave and find a text from Caleb waiting.

Caleb: I hope you had a good day shopping. Are you heading back soon?

My mind goes into a tailspin with what I could possibly say to get out of having to go back for dinner. Each time I start typing out my response, I quickly delete it, second-guessing myself. As uncomfortable as this is, it doesn't even compare to what it would be if I joined them tonight.

> Me: Shopping was fun, but I'm back at the hotel with a horrible migraine. I don't think I'll be able to make it.

It's a little white lie—sure I did have a migraine, but the medicine has relieved me of the pain. Regardless, there's no way I'm going, so I brace myself for his response, praying he'll be understanding.

> Caleb: The chef has been here preparing everything for the past hour. What do you mean you aren't going to come?

> Me: I can barely lift my head off the pillow. I feel awful because I know your parents put a lot into this dinner, but there is no way I can make it. Please tell them how sorry I am.

I hate that I'm putting him in this position, but all I want to do is erase this day and forget it ever happened. I sit in bed and wait for his response, wait for the phone to ring, wait for anything.

Nothing comes.

How did this trip, which was going so perfect, turn into a nightmare?

I nearly bleed my lip from biting it so much as I contemplate sending another text, I talk myself into it and out of it a dozen times before the door to the suite opens.

The moment he walks into the room, our eyes lock. "I thought you couldn't lift your head off the pillow?"

His question requires me to lie, so I avoid it entirely and ask my own as I take in the cut on his cheek, which is slightly bruised and scabbed over. "How did you get back here?"

"I took a cab." With a bold stature, he takes another step closer, intimidating me when he asks, "Are you lying to me?"

His question sounds more like an accusation, which completely unnerves me. All I can do is stare at him and shake my head. Lost is the tender and sweet man I've come to love.

"Then what's the problem? Hurry up and get dressed."

"Caleb—" My voice trembles when I finally find it, and I press my lips together to keep them from wobbling.

He doesn't let me finish before he starts yelling. "Do you have any idea the embarrassment you will cause me? My parents are expecting you tonight. After all the thought and consideration my mother has put into this dinner—for *you*."

"But—"

"The lack of respect it would show if you don't come would be a slap in their faces."

"I'm not trying to be disrespectful at all. I really don't feel good."

"It's a headache," he says as if it's nothing. "Pop an aspirin."

And yeah, it isn't a full-blown migraine, but he doesn't know that. The way he's dismissing me, not even asking how I'm feeling, is really upsetting. Everything about the way he's acting toward me is so out of character for him.

His hands curl into fists, and he paces the room as if he's caged or too angry to stand still. "I'm putting my neck on the line for you, and this is how you act?"

"What's that supposed to mean?"

"You aren't the typical girl I would bring home—you're nothing like what they expect from me, but I chose not to hide you away."

His words are a sucker punch, impaling me right into my self-worth. "Then why even bring me here?"

"If I knew you were going to act this ungrateful, I wouldn't have."

Confused as to who this Caleb is, I'm dumbfounded when I ask, "Why are you doing this? Why are you treating me this way?"

"I could ask you the same thing. You say you care about me, but all I see is you being selfish right now."

"How could you even question that? Of course, I care about you."

"Then get dressed."

"Look at us; we're fighting!" I exclaim. "I really don't think this is a good idea."

"But disrespecting me, not to mention, my family, is?" He slings his words at me, his tone edging on spiteful.

"You know that isn't true, but . . . I don't think tonight is—"

"Is what?" he snaps.

Shifting on the bed, I sit on my knees and clasp my jittery hands together before looking him dead on. "What happened this morning scared me."

His jaw clenches. "I don't know what you think you saw, but you clearly have misunderstood the situation."

"Misunderstood?" Is he crazy? How could I have misunderstood when I'm staring at the cut on his face.

"You know nothing about my life, and I don't expect you to understand it, but that doesn't change the fact that I want you in it."

"And I want to be in it. I just don't think this is a good idea—not tonight."

"It must be so easy for you. Your life is yours. My life isn't," he says.

His statement contradicts everything he's told me. He left Chicago to start a life on his own despite his parents' views. And now, here he is, insinuating something entirely different. "I don't understand. You've always been so adamant about walking away from all their pressure, so what's changed?" I ask. "Is it your dad? Is that what your fight was about this morning?"

"I'm not discussing this right now. I need you to go pull yourself together."

"No," I state firmly. "I'm not going."

His expression morphs into stone, and I swear it isn't Caleb I'm looking at when he seethes, "Get your ass out of bed and get ready."

"Don't talk to me like that!" I yell, my anger boiling.

"Don't act like an infantile bitch then!" he spits before turning on his heel and throwing his fist into the wall so hard he busts right through it, sending plaster to the floor.

White-hot fear lances me, and I turn cold as pieces of my love for him chip into shards that free fall into the pit of stomach.

I watch in horror as he walks to the closet, rips one of my dresses off the hanger, and stalks over to me. He comes quickly and with such anger that I coil back when he grabs my arm and yanks me off the bed. His fingers bite into my skin, and I wince as he drags me to the bathroom.

"Caleb, stop!" I cry out. "Let go of me!"

The moment we hit the threshold, he shoves me in and I fall to the floor, clipping my shoulder against the doorjamb and landing hard on my hipbone. He then slings the dress at me with so much force it stings as it slaps me across my face.

"Get dressed. It isn't a choice."

He slams the door so hard it rattles the mirror above the sink.

Terror washes over me like hot wax as I climb to my feet and backstep away from the door. Tears flood my eyes, blurring my vision before spilling down my cheeks. My body is strangled in shock. Pressing myself against the wall, I question if this is a bad dream because this can't be real.

The pain radiating in my shoulder tells me it is, and when I turn my head and see the lash of red blooming on my skin, I grow angry.

My breathing picks up, and I'm forced to bite my lips together to keep myself from losing my shit on him. I'm too scared of what his reaction will be if I storm out of here and tell him to fuck off. I can't trust that he won't do something worse. Even though he just grabbed me, an hour ago I never would have been able to imagine him putting a hand on me in anger.

Suddenly, everything has changed. I don't know who that guy is on the other side of this door, but what I do know is that I'm petrified of him.

Taking in a few deep breathes while I figure out what to do. My mind scrambles before going to Ady. I need to call her, tell her what's going on because I want nothing more than to go home right now. I calm down enough to remember my phone is on the nightstand by the bed. Somehow, I manage to get my bearings enough to walk over to the door. Unsure if he's still in the bedroom, I slowly turn the nob and peek out to find the space empty. My eyes go straight to the nightstand, and I swear the wind is instantly knocked out of me when I find my phone is gone.

Stepping back, I lock myself away and resign to the fact that I'm powerless right now. He has me stuck, but after tonight, I'm gone.

Fuck this guy.

Sixteen

KATE

THERE'S BEEN NO PHYSICAL CONTACT AT ALL SINCE CALEB AND I left the hotel. Not that I want any. I'm so angry that I can barely look at him as he drives to his parents' place. The self-control it's taking not to lose my shit on him is monumental. Irritation stirs inside me, and when he reaches over the console to take my hand, I jerk it away.

His eyes narrow. "Are you going to be like this all night?"

"Are you going to give me back my phone?" I snap.

"I told you, I don't have it. It isn't my problem you can't keep up with your things."

The audacity of him is downright asinine. "Then, yeah, I guess I'm going to be like this all night."

His grip on the steering wheel strengthens, turning his knuckles white as we make the last turn that takes us into the parking garage. When he parks and unfastens his seatbelt, he warns, "Don't embarrass me," before stepping out.

Stubborn, I sit, not wanting to leave this car because not only am I angry but I'm also scared and nervous and heartbroken. Who is this guy?

After a moment, he opens the door and holds out his hand for me to take, but all I do is stare at it, unsure if I should give in to his offering.

When he sees my hesitation, he drops to his haunches and meets me at eye level. Leaving his harsh tone behind, he gently touches my knee, saying, "Please . . . I don't want to fight with you."

And I don't want to fight with him. I never wanted that, but this isn't on me. I'm not the one to blame.

"Look, I'm sorry I lost my cool back at the hotel, and I know you're pissed, but I can't have my parents seeing this tension between us," he says.

Lost his cool? He didn't just lose his cool, he lost his mind.

Turning away, I look at his hand as he lightly strokes it along my knee—the same hand he used to drag me across a room and toss me into the bathroom. I want to shove it away, but I don't because it will only make this worse. Instead, I give in, but only for dinner tonight. After, I'm packing my things and going back home.

"Fine," I clip before allowing him to help me out of the car.

I stride next to him, the sound of my heels bite into the concrete and echo through the garage. He leads me inside and onto the elevator, and I stand next to him while focusing on the floor and waiting for him to press the button.

Instead, he lifts my chin and angles me to look at him. "I promise, I'll make this up to you."

"There is no making up for what you did."

His expression falls, but the tension around his eyes remains, exposing the nerves I know he has about tonight. Wanting to get this over with, I reach out and push the button myself. As we ascend, his palm sweats against mine, but he does well with keeping his composure. He stands tall in his designer suit, staring at the floor numbers above the door as they light up, one by one, until we come to a stop.

After a quick adjustment of his tie, he holds my hand and leads me toward what I'm sure will be a disastrous dinner.

I can't believe this situation I've found myself in. This morning, we woke up and everything was great—everything was fine. Now . . . now I feel like I'm holding on to a stranger's hand.

"There you are," his mother croons when we arrive.

Caleb's hand doesn't leave mine when she pulls us both in for a hug.

"Come on in. I just popped into the kitchen, and Nigel is almost ready to serve the first course."

I smile, not wanting to be rude to her. "It smells amazing."

"His food tastes even better. Trust me."

We follow her into the formal dining room where his father is already sitting and enjoying whatever brown liquor is in his lowball. "Ah, you made it," he says when he lifts his attention from his phone.

His voice is a thorn in my side, and when he stands to greet me with a sweeping kiss to my cheek, a flashing memory of seeing him hit Caleb flits through me.

"Please have a seat."

Stepping around the table to the place settings meant for Caleb and me, I watch as the two of them hug and Conrad pats a fatherly hand against Caleb's back. The affection scathes me, and for a split second, I soften toward Caleb when I consider how many times his father has hit him in the past.

When he sits next to me, I feel the need to show a sign of comfort toward him, but the dull throb in my shoulder is enough to still my hand.

Rose settles next to Conrad and drapes her napkin across her lap. "Kate, how was your day? What fabulous things did you buy?"

For a moment, truth and lies tangle along my tongue, but I'm saved when a lady walks into the room, holding a bottle of wine in each hand.

"Would you care for some wine?"

"Oh, no thanks," I respond despite wanting the alcohol to help get me through this dinner.

"You should try the cabernet," Conrad suggests. "I had a glass earlier, and it was quite good. Not too sweet."

Since he doesn't seem to frown on underage drinking, I hold out my glass, not that I needed his permission. It isn't as if I'm ever going to see him again after tonight anyway. I take a sip while the lady pours a glass for Caleb and Rose.

"So . . . your day of shopping . . ." Rose says, picking up on her previous question.

"It was good. I didn't buy anything, but it was fun to browse."

From beneath the table, Caleb touches my leg before I nudge his hand away.

"I'll make sure to buy her something nice before we leave," he tells his mother.

Her eyes brighten at the idea. "Yes, something to remember this trip by."

My only hope is to dissolve this trip from my memory. I certainly don't want a memento.

Conrad clears his throat in a way meant to garner attention before saying, "Your mother told me the two of you visited Cascade Falls." His eyes shift to me. "That's where I proposed to Rose."

"It's beautiful there," I respond, feeling like a puppet in this shit show.

I'm surprised this table isn't wobbling with all the crap these people shove under the rug. It was only hours ago that Conrad hit Caleb and that Rose saw me running out here, and far less than that since Caleb threw me to the floor like a piece of garbage. I can't even wrap my mind around the craziness today has held as I watch the three of them act like everything is peachy keen.

It's crazy.

When the chef enters the room, I thank God for the distraction and take another sip of my wine as Nigel presents the first course, which consists of a light balsamic-infused watermelon salad.

I eat slowly to busy myself as Conrad talks to Caleb about some new construction development in the city one of his clients is an investor of. With so much confusion swimming in my head, I'm too distracted to pay attention, but I smile and nod along as if I am.

As one course ends and another begins, Caleb attempts another display of affection when he leans back in his chair and runs his hand along my shoulder. It's most likely the glass of wine I just finished that keeps me from pushing him away. Not that I would do that in front of his parents. Despite how he treated me earlier, I'm not a total bitch.

His thumb brushes along my tender skin, which is now tinged in a faint bruise, and when I meet his eyes, he gives a soft smile, one I refuse to return. He lifts his hand and attempts to run the back of his finger along the side of my face, and it's now that I reject him and turn away. His parents don't see as they eat their duck carpaccio.

Caleb scoots his chair back.

"Everything all right, dear?"

He acknowledges his mother as he stands. "Yes, I'm just going to excuse myself for a moment. I'll be right back."

I didn't think I could possibly feel any more uncomfortable, but being alone with his parents is a whole new level of hell for me.

Conrad is fairly quiet for the most part while Rose makes

small talk about how good the food is. "We hired Nigel for a dinner party we hosted for some close friends. He made an amazing corn ice cream using dry ice."

"Corn ice cream?"

She laughs. "I flipped my nose too, but it had to have been the best ice cream I've ever tasted."

"Corn has no place being in desserts," Conrad scoffs as she shakes her head at him.

The chef's assistant clears our plates, and Caleb still hasn't returned.

"More wine?" his father offers, and when I nod, he picks up the bottle, leans forward, and fills my glass.

I take a sip, but tell myself not to go overboard. My cheeks are already flushed with heat, and even though I need to take the edge off, I don't want to get drunk.

Caleb walks back into the room. "Sorry that took so long."

Time passes slowly through the next two courses, and when the last one is finally served, my anticipation blooms, knowing that this night is almost over. I fake a yawn in hopes to make an early exit.

"Long day?" Rose asks with a caring smile on her lips.

"I'm sorry. I don't mean to be rude."

"Not at all. The two of you have been busy this week." She sets her spoon down next to her half-eaten pot de crème. "Why don't you take her back to the hotel, Caleb? I can see you're tired too."

"Are you sure, Mom. I hate to eat and run."

"Nonsense." His father wipes his mouth with his napkin and tosses it onto the table. "It's been a long day for all of us, and I have a few phone calls I need to make."

"Dinner was lovely, thank you so much," I tell them.

"It was our pleasure." Rose rounds the table and hugs me.

In a strange way, I feel sorry for this woman in the same way I would feel sorry for a trapped animal. She appears content and happy, but if Conrad is so willing to hit his son, I doubt that he has restraint with his wife.

As Caleb is driving us back to the hotel, a fresh rush of panic swims through my veins when I think about what I'm about to do. I begin praying that he won't lose his temper like he did before when I tell him I'm going home tonight. I don't even know if there are any flights left, but I don't care. I'll sleep in the airport if I have to.

I peer over at him, and he seems calm. Come to think of it, he's been pretty quiet all night—almost broody. Maybe he feels bad for how he behaved earlier . . . not that it matters to me if he does.

When we make it to our floor in the hotel, my neck breaks out in a cold sweat, and I fidget as I wait for Caleb to pull out the keycard and unlock the door, and when he finally opens it, I stand frozen in utter shock. Unable to move as I look inside, my mouth gapes in surprise. His hand meets my lower back as he guides me into the candle-lit room drenched in flowers. The door closes behind us, and I'm stunned.

Massive blooms of white and every shade of pink roses span the entire space. I inhale a lungful of fragrance, and when Caleb takes my hand in his, I turn toward him. Sadness paints his eyes as he stares into mine. His shoulders sag in dejection, and his voice is a mere whisper when he tells me, "I'm sorry."

Pain is clear in his expression as the candlelight flickers around the room, and the moment I see tears building along his bottom lashes, he hangs his head.

"Caleb."

"I'm so sorry." His words crack beneath his apology, and when he looks at me, I see how broken up he is. "I don't know what happened." His hands cup my cheeks and there isn't a single urge to push him away. Instead, I slip my hands around his wrists when he drops his forehead to mine. "I can't believe I did that, but I promise you"—he pulls back to face me straight on—"it will *never* happen again. I swear to you." His forehead comes back to mine. "I hate myself for what I did."

"Don't say that."

"My emotions overpowered me when I felt like you were judging me."

"I wasn't judging you at all," I try to assure him.

He then takes my hand and leads me over to the sofa where we sit. His brows furrow as if he's in the middle of some internal struggle.

"What is it?"

He takes my hands in his, lifts his sorrowful eyes to mine, and finally gives me what I've been waiting for when he confesses, "I love you."

A breath of elation escapes me, and I smile.

"I've been in love with you for a while, I was just scared to tell you because I have a hard time trusting people. Trusting women."

Happiness falls from my lips but remains in my heart. "Why?"

With a slight shake of his head, he says, "Growing up here, my name meant something—it still does, and people know it. Especially the people I went to school with. There was a girl I dated for two years. I fell hard for her, and I believed her completely when she told me she loved me. The night of our graduation, I overheard her telling a friend of hers that she was basically only tolerating me because she wanted the life of a Bradford."

"She used you," I murmur.

"She then went on to tell her the things I had only ever

opened up to her about, mocking me and laughing behind my back."

I squeeze his hands, and my heart breaks more for this man. "I'm so sorry."

"Being used by people who want a taste of my life isn't anything new. It's one of the reasons I moved. But then I met you." He strokes his fingers through my hair lovingly. "You're so far from pretentious that I couldn't help myself from falling in love with you."

He says the words again, and I swear they cause my heart to swell in my chest.

"I was excited to bring you here. I felt safe to show you where I came from because I knew you wouldn't get swept away by the money—you aren't that type of girl." He chuckles under his breath. "You're a hard one to impress."

I gaze around the room, telling him, "This impresses me." And then my focus comes back to him. "*You* impress me."

"I thought you were ready to run when you wanted to bail on my family tonight," he tells me. "I thought that when you saw the home I grew up in and . . . everything else that it was too much for you and that you didn't want to be with someone like me."

"That wasn't it at all."

"I got scared because I let myself fall for you, and I thought I was going to lose you."

"Caleb, no," I assure as I move in closer. "Does all the extravagance make me a little uncomfortable? Yes, but I would never let that deter my feelings for you. I love you," I reveal before adding, "This morning just . . . it scared me. I didn't know what to do." I lift my fingers and drag them along the broken flesh on his cheekbone. Tears flood my eyes, and my voice slips when I say it again, "I didn't know what to do."

He takes my face in his hands and kisses me with so much love that I feel like I might burst. It erases all my anger and fear from earlier and replaces it with warmth that I want to curl against and keep forever. I know that when I look back on this night, I won't remember our fight because this, this right here makes up for all of that.

"I never meant to hurt you, I need you to believe me when I tell you that," he breathes against my lips.

"I know." There isn't a single part of me that doesn't believe him. For Caleb to be this torn up and vulnerable . . . how could anyone question his remorse? There's a pain inside him, a torment I can feel, that's begging for me to reach out and heal it. A torment no one has been able to get to, but I will. "I forgive you," I tell him, and he breathes a heavy sigh of relief when he gathers me into his arms.

His embrace is fierce, and I hug him back. When his lips press softly against the bruise on my shoulder, I begin to cry, but not for me—it's for him. He's wounded in a way I never knew, but now I do, and I won't let one bad night tear me away from him.

Seventeen

KATE

"HOW ARE YOU SETTLING IN TO YOUR NEW PLACE?" MY DAD asks as he passes me a dinner roll.

"Everything is good. I mean . . . it's weird living on my own, and it's been a little lonely."

My mom stabs her fork into her salad a few times, saying, "I'm sure it won't feel too lonely once Caleb gets back to town, plus classes are about to start back up."

"Yeah. It's been really quiet this summer."

Caleb was supposed to come back to Miami with me, but he decided to stay in Chicago with his parents for a little longer. It's been just over two weeks since I came home, and the time without him has been lonely, and I can't wait to see him when he flies back tonight. I miss him.

"Tell us," my mom says as we sit around the dining table and eat dinner. "When do we get to meet this boy?"

"I don't know."

"Do you have a picture of him?" my little sister asks with hearts in her eyes, curious as to how cute he is.

With a roll of my eyes, I toss her my cell phone, and she's quick to drop her fork and open my photo album. My mother leans in as they scroll through a few of the pics I took while I was in Chicago. I shake my head as the two of them gush.

"Let me see that," my father says, snatching the phone from them. He swipes through a few photos before glancing up at me. "You told him I carry a gun, right?"

"Dad."

He hands the phone back to me. "He better be treating you right."

"He is," I assure. "He comes from a good family too." I say it more out of reflex than the need to tell the truth. Sure, Rose is a lovely person, but nothing could convince me that she isn't a victim herself or ignorant to how Caleb's father treats him.

My dad gives an approving nod, so I let it go and turn to my sister. "What's up with you and Zach?"

Audrina glances at Dad, and he raises his fork with a piece of steak dangling off the prongs as he points it in her direction. "That boy is bad news."

"You're so annoying."

"What happened?" I ask.

"Nothing," she exclaims before my dad can respond.

"It isn't nothing."

I look between the three of them. "Will someone just tell me?"

"Be nice," my mother murmurs, resting her hand over my dad's.

"The kid can't tell time."

"It wasn't his fault, Dad."

"Boys that age have nothing but bad intentions," he tells her, and I shove a piece of steak into my mouth to keep from laughing.

He used to say the same thing to me when I was still living at home.

"Why do you just assume that every guy is a pervert?"

"Because they are."

"Honey, stop," my mom gently chastises.

"Kate, do you want to know what he did?" Audrina huffs. "He showed up to the party I was at in his patrol car! He was still in uniform when he walked right in and escorted me out like I was a criminal. He did it in front of *everyone*. It was humiliating!"

Dad smiles proudly. "I'd do it again."

"You're unbelievable."

"He did the same thing to me junior year."

Dad grumbles. "I don't even want to remember that night."

"How did I not hear about this?" she questions, and Dad goes on to tell her, "I showed up to a house party your sister was at and she couldn't even walk out because she was so drunk."

My sister looks at me in shock and then turns to our parents. "Are you serious? Why are you coming down on me so hard then? I wasn't even drinking."

"You got off easy compared to your sister."

"I was grounded for three weeks," I tell her. "But even worse, I woke up the next morning with my first hangover, and he made me go outside in the blistering heat and, not only wash but also wax both cars. I can't count how many times I barfed in the shrubs."

"Kate," my mother snaps in disgust. "I'm trying to eat my dinner."

"Blame Dad."

"I'm not raising delinquents here." It's his only explanation, and my sister and I roll our eyes.

After we finish dinner, I help my mom clear the table and load the dishwasher before rushing out to get back to Miami.

Anxious to see Caleb, I busy myself around my new apartment. He texted me a little while ago to tell me his plane had landed and that he was headed my way. When he knocks and I answer, I give him a big hug before helping him drag his luggage inside.

156

"What's this?" I ask when he sets a bag from Magnolia Bakery in front of me.

"Dessert."

I smile, excited to see what he brought me back from Chicago. While I was there, I fell in love with this bakery. Their confections are out of this world, and when I open the pastry box and find a half dozen truffle cupcakes, I immediately dip my finger into the ganache and lick it off.

"Oh my god." I moan, rolling my head back in chocolate ecstasy.

"If only you made those noises for me," he teases before planting a kiss along my neck.

I carry the pastry box into the living room as he takes a quick look around the new apartment.

"How did the move go?"

"It was good," I tell him.

He comes to sit next to me on the couch. "I'm sorry I couldn't be here to help."

"Don't worry about it." He slips his arm around me and kisses me, slower and longer this time, and when I draw back, I whisper, "How was the rest of your stay?"

"It was good," he answers with a slight grin, echoing my response about the move. "My mother adores you."

His sentiment is sweet, but I don't miss that his father wasn't included in that statement.

"I really like her too." I am also appalled by her and her complicity. "Are they still pushing you to move back home after graduation?"

"Yeah."

Caleb moving away tears my heart because I love him and I don't want to lose him, but I also don't want to be "that" girl, so I smile and tilt my head to drop another slow kiss on his lips.

"You mind if I get out of these clothes?" he asks, his breath feathering across my skin as he speaks.

"No, go ahead."

He takes one of his suitcases into my bedroom, and I follow him in, sitting on the bed while he changes into a pair of athletic shorts and a T-shirt. After he folds his jeans, he walks over to the dresser to set them down and picks up my pen I left out and turns to me.

Caleb holds the pen in his fingers and examines it for a beat before he comes over, sits next to me on the bed, and hands it over.

"Can I be honest with you about something?"

"Of course," I tell him.

He shifts and faces me straight on. "I've tried to be okay with the fact that you use this stuff, but I'm not going to lie . . . it really bothers me."

"I have a med card. I'm not doing anything illegal."

"I know you aren't, but it's the stigma that still surrounds pot." He takes my hand in his. "The last thing I want is for people to judge you based on this, but that's the reality. They will judge you regardless of how benign you say it is."

I've known since almost the start that he isn't comfortable around pot, and even though I don't see the problem, I love him enough that I don't want to do anything that's going to make him uncomfortable. It's been months since he found out, and he hasn't said a word, not even when I do it in front of him.

"Do you understand where I'm coming from, babe?"

"I do," I tell him. "I just didn't know it bugged you so much."

"I didn't want to say anything and upset you." His tone is marked tenderly with caution, as if he thinks I'm going to fly off the handle. It's cute that he doesn't understand the basic characteristics of a pot smoker. We're pretty chill people.

158

There is a second where I weigh my appreciation for smoking against how much his feelings mean to me before responding, "If you don't want me to use it anymore, I won't."

"You'd do that for me?"

"I love you, and the last thing I want to do is make you uncomfortable," I tell him before reaching over and opening the drawer to my nightstand. I pull out the cartridge boxes and hand them over to him, along with the pen. "Here."

"Are you sure?"

I nod. "I wouldn't be doing it if I weren't okay with it. I promise. Go ahead and throw them away."

There's a hint of relief in his expression, which I'm glad to see, before he walks into the kitchen to toss them into the trash. The last thing this man needs is more stress in his life, so if my stopping will make him happy, I will.

When he returns, he's grinning and has a small rectangular box in his hand. He crawls onto the bed next to me and holds the box out for me to take.

"What is this?"

"Open it and see."

Slowly, I push the top back to reveal the cushion-cut diamond that hangs from a delicately thin platinum chain. "Caleb," I whisper. "I can't accept this."

"You don't like it?"

Not like it? Has he lost his mind? It's beautiful. "That's not it at all. I love it."

"So what's the problem?"

"It's too nice," I tell him, and he laughs. "I'm serious," I exclaim. "I couldn't possibly take this from you."

He gently pulls the necklace from the box. "You aren't taking anything." Unclasping the chain, he leans over and secures it around my neck. "I'm giving it to you because I want you to know how much you mean to me." His hands slide along my cheeks as he pulls me to him, kissing me so deeply, so passionately, that my whole body warms in his touch. "I've never met anyone like you."

"Is that a good thing?" I murmur teasingly, and when he lowers me back onto the bed, he smiles and affirms, "It's the best thing."

Slowly, piece-by-piece, we strip down until we're skin on skin, and then we make love. With his diamond resting in the hollow of my throat, my heart settles into his heart, and there's no place I'd rather be than tucked beneath him as we move together. Despite what happened in Chicago, there's no doubt that this is the real Caleb. That, in this moment, I can see right through to the core of who he is and who he's meant to be. Beyond that, nothing else matters.

Eighteen

TRENT

FIRST SEMESTER OF SOPHOMORE YEAR STARTED A COUPLE OF WEEKS ago. This year is nothing like last, and it's been bumming me out. Micah and Ady are a thing, which was bound to happen, but it's totally shifted the whole dynamic of the condo. On top of that, Kate has been MIA, off doing her thing with her boyfriend. And then there's my mom. She's moving forward with the divorce, and surprisingly, the drama on her end has died down—for the moment.

"Are you heading out?" Ady asks as I toss a bottle of sunscreen into my backpack.

Micah had a photoshoot for one of his sponsor's new apparel lines and is down at one of the small local beaches. I told him I'd meet him there afterward.

"Yeah. What do you have going on?"

She looks at her cell phone before dropping it to her side. "I was trying to get ahold of Kate to see if she wanted to hang out."

"No luck?"

She shakes her head. "Have you heard from her at all lately?"

Tossing a few bottles of water into my bag, I shake my head. "No, man. I haven't seen her at all."

The last time I even spoke to Kate was at a party right before summer. Micah told me she was who brought me home that night, but I have absolutely zero memory of it. That was months ago, and it's strange for her not to be around all the time anymore. She hasn't even come out surfing with the crew, and if she has, it hasn't been when I was around.

As I zip up my bag, Ady takes a seat at the kitchen island, seemingly annoyed.

"What's bothering you, sis?"

"Nothing," she murmurs almost listlessly. "It's just . . . am I the only one seeing a change in her since she and Caleb got serious?"

"How serious are they?"

Her eyes stretch in disbelief. "Have you not the seen the diamond?"

A sledgehammer barrels into my chest. "What the fuck are you talking about?"

"He bought her this insanely expensive diamond necklace," she says, and I breathe a sigh of relief that it wasn't a damn ring. "In my book, that isn't something you buy the person you're casually dating."

The thought of that pretentious punk scathes me. I've never liked his vibe at all, but I get what Ady is dropping. She isn't the same Kate she was before Caleb came into the picture.

After slinging the backpack over my shoulders, I grab my skimboard, muttering, "Seems like a waste of time to me."

"On who's end?"

"On both of theirs."

"They love each other."

"Whatever you say," I respond before grabbing my things and heading out.

When I get down to my SUV and toss my bag and board into the back, I shoot a quick text to Micah.

Me: You done? I'm heading out now.

Micah: Almost. We packed up to hit another location, but I'll be back that way in about 20 minutes.

When I make it to the beach, there are only a few other cars in the parking lot. The swells are lacking, making it near impossible to surf, but I enjoy skimming more. The sand is practically deserted with only a few people scattered about. It's a short distance of beach between the parking lot and the water, and I waste no time, dropping my backpack and hopping on my board.

With the morning sun on my skin and salt in my hair, I jump the small waves, throwing down a few tricks as I wait on Micah. I'm not in the water for too long before I catch his truck pulling into a spot.

"What's up?" I shout from the water, watching as he grabs his board and jogs my way. "How did the shoot go, pretty boy?"

He elbows me in the ribs. "Don't give me shit, man."

"Did I hit a nerve?"

"Fuck off."

We laugh as we walk down to the shore. I break Micah's balls often, but it's all in love. He's made a name for himself in the local surf scene, and I'm proud of the guy. As we waste away the morning doing what we do best, a few guys join us in the water. It's nothing but varial flips, back threes, and shiftys. We ride the mellow water, and when I ass slide off a kickflip, everyone razzes me.

"Pow! Right in the kisser." Micah laughs.

Grabbing my board, I slick my hand through my hair as I brush off the wipeout. "Nothing like chaffing the angel."

With a careless grin, I leave everyone in the water, drop my board next to my bag, and look up just in time to spot Kate out of the corner of my eye. She and fucking Caleb are standing next to his douche-bag worthy car talking. The stucco wall from the showers obstructs my line of vision, but from what I can see, it looks like they're arguing.

I'm surprised to even see her here when we haven't crossed paths in months, but whatever her reason is for showing up today, I'd rather lick a dick than have to share the water with that cocknard.

"Yo," I yell to Micah. "I'm bailing."

"What the hell, man?"

"I'll catch you back at the condo."

Shouting from the parking lot pulls my attention, and when I look over my shoulder, Caleb is in her face with his hand clutched around her arm. A roiling of anger spikes inside me, and I quickly grab my board and bag, but by the time I make it within earshot of them, he's already heading in my direction and down to the sand.

"What the fuck, dude?" I sneer as we pass each other, but he gives me no response.

Kate remains at his car, leaning against it with her back facing me. She doesn't notice as I walk toward her, so I have a second to take in her splotchy, tear-stained face without her trying to hide it.

"What the hell is going on?"

She quickly wipes her tears, appearing shocked to see me. "What are you doing here?"

"Skimming with the guys," I respond before asking for a second time, "What the hell is going on?"

"What do you mean?"

I step in front of her so I can keep my eyes on the beach, and I don't miss when Caleb glances our way. He looks pissed, so I shoot him an air kiss.

Kate shoves my shoulder hard enough for me to almost take a step back. "Stop being a dick to him."

"We need to talk," I tell her, taking her hand and walking her behind the shower wall so Caleb can't see us anymore. "Why the fuck did he just grab you?" Not that any reason she could ever give for why he did it would be good enough.

"What are you talking about?"

I take her elbow in my hand, and when she looks at her arm, I snap, "This is what I'm talking about."

She jerks out of my hold. "He didn't grab me," she defends, but it's bullshit.

"I *saw* him grab you, so stop lying to me."

There's a subtle shift in her eyes that exposes a crack in her façade, and it punches me in the gut.

"Has he done that before?"

"He didn't *do* anything." She tries to lie again, but it falls on deaf ears.

"I know what I saw."

"Apparently, you don't."

The fact that she can hardly look at me pisses me off. Her lying to me pisses me off even more, and I know she can see it written all over my face.

"What do you even see in that guy?"

She huffs and starts walking away, muttering, "I'm not doing this with you."

In three quick strides, I'm back in front of her, stopping her dead in her tracks. "I'm serious. Any man who puts his hands on you isn't worth your time. I know what I saw, whether you want to admit it or not, and the fingerprints on your arm are proof enough that I'm not mistaken. That guy is a piece of ass shit."

"Suddenly, you're the expert on relationships?" She fake

laughs. "How rich coming from *you*. You've never even been in a relationship because you're too scared."

"That's a fuckin' low blow."

"Yeah? Well, so is half the shit you say to me."

Stepping closer to her, I take a slow breath in an attempt to better compose myself because the last thing I want to do is upset her any more than she already is.

"I'm sorry," I give her softly. "You're right, I'm not an expert on relationships, but I'd be lying if I said a part of me wasn't worried about you."

Her brows cinch in confusion, but I don't think she's confused at all. I think she knows exactly what I'm talking about.

"You have no reason to be worried," she says. "Couples argue all the time, but for you to insinuate that Caleb is anything other than a good man is crossing the line."

"Is it? Then why can't you look at me and say that?"

She shrugs.

My eyes drift off as I shake my head.

"You haven't liked Caleb from the moment you met him, but that has nothing to do with me."

Her point is on the mark, but my distaste for the guy only increases with each day she ghosts her friends and each excuse she makes for him. After seeing him grab her, there's no way I'm going to able to be cool with him.

My eyes fall from hers, landing on the diamond around her neck. Ady was right, it's too much, and it's all wrong. I can't control my disgust, and I take a step back from her. "He doesn't know you at all, does he?"

Her hand slowly rises to her necklace, and she fiddles the diamond between her fingers.

"It doesn't fit who you are," I tell her.

"Maybe you're the one who doesn't know me."

"Is that why you're with him? Because he has deep pockets?"

"Fuck you, Trent," she snaps, her hand falling from her neck.

Her face is red with anger as she turns on her heel and walks off.

This time, I let her go, watching as she makes her way down the beach to where Caleb is talking to Micah. Even though he just put a mark on her, she doesn't hesitate before she slips her arm around his waist and sidles up next to him as if nothing happened.

Nineteen

KATE

As I stand in front of the three-way mirror, I run my hands along the smooth fabric of the floor-length dress with a tasteful slit up the thigh and the sleek one-shoulder neckline.

I look at my mother's reflection in the glass and seek her approval. "What do you think?"

"It's perfect." She smiles as she gathers my hair and pulls it away from my face and neck. "I'm wondering if you should wear your hair up tonight."

"I don't have time to get into a stylist," I tell her. "I'll just wear it down in loose curls."

"Next time, don't wait until hours before an event to figure all this out. I'm shocked you aren't stressed about having to find a dress so last minute."

"Oh, I'm stressed, but I think I found the dress."

The sales associate comes to check on me, smiling approvingly of how well it fits.

"I think this will work."

"Will you be needing any alterations?"

"She doesn't have time for alterations," my mother tells the lady. "We will take it as is."

I step down from the small platform and head back to the

fitting room. Tonight is the annual Luminocity Charity Gala in Fort Lauderdale, and since I've never been to a black-tie event before, I was excited when Caleb invited me. Then he told me his parents would be flying in for the occasion, and I started to dread it. Apparently, his father is a major donor to this particular organization, which is the largest in the country and raises money for ovarian cancer research, the very illness Conrad lost his mother to.

If it weren't for my mother's willingness to drop everything and drive to Miami to help me find a dress, I wouldn't stand a chance at getting Conrad to change his mind about me.

"Here you go," I say, handing the merlot-colored dress to the sales clerk.

"What about shoes?" my mom asks as we walk to the cash registers.

"I was thinking I would wear my black Stuart Weitzman heels with the ankle strap."

She nods in approval, taking my hand and giving it an enthusiastic squeeze. "You're going to have so much fun," she says as she hands over her credit card to pay for the dress. "You're lucky to have found a guy like Caleb who comes from a prominent and well-respected family."

I smile because I do feel lucky to have Caleb in my life.

"I wish I could've met him today."

"I know, but he's at the hotel with his parents right now."

Once the purchase has been made, the clerk zips the dress into a garment bag and hands it to me. "Thank you."

The humidity hits hard when we step out into the late September heat, and as we walk to her car, I ask, "Do you have time to help me get ready?"

"I wish I did, dear. I was able to reschedule my showings, but I have a closing that I need to get back for."

Slipping into the car, she pegs the AC, and starts driving me back to my condo. "I really appreciate you driving all this way to help me find a dress."

"Nonsense. I really enjoyed stealing this time with you." As she battles the Miami traffic back to my building, she goes on to tell me, "I'm so happy for you. Caleb seems like quite a catch."

"You say that as if you're surprised I could snag a guy like him."

She smirks. "Not surprised, dear, just . . ."

Her thought drifts off as she searches for the right word, and I start laughing. "Oh my god! You are surprised, aren't you?"

She joins in on the humor. "Okay, yes. I'm surprised. I mean, you spend half your days on a board with sand in your hair. I just figured you'd find yourself with some *surfer dude*." She throws up a shaka when she says the last part.

"Don't ever do that again."

"What?"

"Toss up a shaka sign."

"It's what you kids do." She's not wrong, but she still shouldn't do it. It's embarrassing.

After my mom drops me off, I rush up to my place to hop in the shower and start getting ready. As time draws in closer, I take a deep breath and talk myself down from the jitters of having to see Conrad. He's the type of man you walk on eggshells around, and I constantly feel like I'm under his scrutiny when I'm with him. I've never bothered to say anything about it to Caleb because I get the sense that it's the same with him as well.

When Caleb arrives, he looks insanely hot in his tailored tuxedo and black bowtie.

"Maybe we should ditch the gala," I tease with a sinful smile he's quick to kiss.

Wrapping my arms around him, I pull him in tighter, the short scruff on his face lightly grazing against me.

"Don't tempt me," he says when our lips part. "Are you almost ready?"

"Almost."

As I walk back into my bathroom, Caleb sits on my bed while I twist my hair around the barrel of the curling iron. From the corner of my eye, I notice him staring down at his hands, which won't stop wringing. I know better than to ask him if everything is all right. It seems every time he's around his parents, they do nothing but ignite his stress, and I hate that for him. Once I'm done with my hair, I swipe on a little lipstick and spritz on some perfume before we head down to his car.

"You look stunning."

"It isn't too much?" I ask, second-guessing the floor-length dress.

"No, babe. You're perfect," he assures, kissing the back of my hand as he holds it in his.

His rigid grip on me reveals his tension while he drives. Once we arrive in downtown Fort Lauderdale, he navigates through the busy streets that lead us to the event where the local press is set up outside to snap pictures of the city's upper crust.

When Caleb takes my hand and leads me over to the rolled-out black carpet, I pull back.

"What's wrong?"

"Do we have to be photographed?"

Chuckling under his breath, he asks, "What's the big deal?"

"It's weird," I tell him and then lower my voice so those around can't hear when I add, "And super vain."

He plants a kiss on the top of my head. "My father made it clear that I was to be photographed."

"Why?"

"Why do you think? It's publicity."

"Pompous publicity," I joke as he walks me over to stand in front of the logo backdrop where his last name appears scattered about the event name.

It's a nerve-wracking experience to have pictures taken like this, but I swallow my insecurities for Caleb's sake and smile, knowing it isn't me they want pictures of. They only care about the son of the man whose name is splashed all over this event.

I make it through, and he leads me into the building and toward the grand ballroom. The space is dimly lit and dripping in the most lavish flowers I've ever seen. Everyone mingles and sips champagne as a jazz band plays on the stage. In the back of the room, a silent auction is set up, and that's where most people are gathered. It's where Caleb's father is as well, and we make our way over to him.

"There you are, Son." His father grins, clapping his hand on to Caleb's shoulder.

From the outside, you wouldn't suspect anything other than a normal, functioning father-son relationship.

"Kate," he greets me kinder than he has in the past. "Don't you look lovely." Leaning in, he gives me a gentlemanly kiss to my cheek before turning back to Caleb and introducing him to a few older men.

It doesn't take long for Caleb's hand to fall from mine, but a moment later, Rose drifts away from one of the auction tables and joins me. "You made it!" She pulls me in for a hug, warm as always. "It's so good to see you again."

"It's good to see you too."

She then takes my hand, and before I can say anything to Caleb, she pulls me over to where she just came from. "Let's shop!"

I glance around at some of the items up for auction, but

there isn't a thing I can see that I would be comfortable bidding on without first running it by my parents. As the two of us stroll passed items like Botox and liposuction, a weeklong trip to Italy, and an acoustic guitar autographed by Joe Perry, I sneak peeks at the current bids, which are astronomical.

"Whatever you want, dear," she says.

"I'm sorry?"

"To bid on," she clarifies, leaning closer to add, "It's on Conrad's dime tonight."

"Oh, no. I couldn't."

"Don't be silly. This charity is his pride and joy." She then stops in front of a display, featuring a photo of a world-renowned chef who will come to your home and prepare a tasting menu for up to six people. "Look at this! How much fun would this be for you and Caleb and your friends?"

"I don't know." I hesitate, completely uncomfortable spending money that isn't mine, especially Conrad's.

Rose picks up the pen and hands it to me. "I insist."

When I step over to the podium to mark my bid, Rose wanders away, looking at all the other displays. Alone, I look at the bids, and the snarky Kate inside me wants to place a bid that's ten times the amount of the last one listed just to stick it to Conrad. Petty, yes. But it's so very tempting.

Reasonable Kate wins, and I place a modest bid, not wanting my defiance to come back and bite me in the ass. Besides, I don't need to hand him any ammo that might wind up falling on Caleb.

When I'm done filling out the form, I turn and scan the room for Rose, finding her over by the bar, chatting with a few ladies. At this point, I decide to busy myself by browsing through the rest of the auctions, feigning interest to pass time until Caleb finishes with his father.

I pluck a glass of champagne off a tray as a waiter passes and take a sip. As I come to the last item, I open my beaded clutch and pull out my cellphone to check the time. Thirty minutes is all that has passed since arriving. With a bored sigh, I look over my shoulder to see Caleb in deep conversation with an older gentleman. I debate going over there, but then I figure that whatever it is they're discussing is probably more boring than standing idle by myself. So, I kill time and shoot Ady a text.

Me: Hey! What are you up to tonight?

Tucking my clutch under my arm, I take another sip of bubbly as I wait for her to respond, which, luckily, doesn't take too long.

Ady: I'm out with Micah and Trent at the Miami Dolphins game. Micah's dad came across box seat tickets and gave them to us.

Her text is immediately followed by a picture of the three of them, decked out in Miami gear. They look like they're having a blast while I'm stuck—practically alone—at this stuffy gala. Honestly, I'd much rather be drinking beer, eating nachos, and watching the game.

Me: That sounds like so much fun. We should hang out soon. I miss you.

Lazily, I stroll about, politely smiling at people as I pass them, feeling completely out of place in a ballroom that is brimming with over-the-top luxury. It's uncomfortable.

Ady: What about me?

Confused, I stare at the text, wondering what she means when another text pops up.

Ady: It's Trent, btw. Ady is busy murdering the chocolate fountain.
Me: Oh, hey.
Ady: So, what is it? You miss me too or just Ady?

"There you are."

Looking up, I find Caleb standing front of me, and I quickly shove my phone back into my clutch.

"What are you doing?"

"Nothing. Just checking the time."

"Sorry, I kept you waiting for so long."

"It's okay," I tell him, happy to have him next to me. "You should know that your mother practically forced me to bid on one of the auction items."

He chuckles. "I hope you bid high." He then slips his arm around my waist. "Come on, let's dance."

After I set my fluted glass on a random table, Caleb guides me over to the dance floor. With one hand holding mine and his other pressed against my lower back, he leads me as we move to the music.

"Who taught you how to dance like this?"

"My mother."

"I'm impressed."

He smiles down at me, and I swear it's perfect. Tugging me in closer, I rest the side of my head against his cheek as we dance. He keeps a tight hold on me as the band drifts into another song.

"You're quiet," I note, to which he responds, "I have a lot on my mind."

Drawing back, I look into his eyes, imploring him to tell me without my having to outright ask.

"My father introduced me to a former colleague of his that now lives here."

"What did you two talk about?"

The muscles around his shoulder tenses. "I'll tell you another time—not tonight."

He's polite in his refusal to tell me, but that doesn't stop me from wondering what they were speaking about. As the evening moves forward, we eat a lovely dinner, listen to a few cancer survivors tell their stories and offer thanks to the charity, and cheer on the auction winners, of which I am not one.

"Next time, bid higher," Caleb teasingly whispers in my ear.

When everything is said and done, and they have announced how much money the evening raised, a popular band takes the stage for an intimate concert. Soon after they start playing, Conrad and Rose say their goodbyes, and we follow suit.

As Caleb is talking to the valet, I pull out my phone and text Trent back, this time on his cell phone, addressing his last message he sent.

Me: Yes, I miss you too. But, lately, you haven't been the easiest person to be around.

"Let's get back to Miami," Caleb says when he gets into the car. "Did you have a good time?"

"Yeah, it was fun," I tell him as I reach down and unfasten the straps to my heels. "My feet are killing me."

My phone vibrates, and I read the incoming text.

Trent: You're not going to start bustin' my nuts again, are you?

"Who are you talking to?"

"Oh, no one." I brush off Caleb's question as I send another message.

Me: You scared of me?

I place my phone face down on my lap and rest my head back. Through a deep yawn, I mutter, "I'm so tired. I had no idea it was going to last so long." When he doesn't say anything, I run my hand along his shoulder and sit up when I find it's rock hard with tension. "Is everything okay?"

He gives a curt nod, but before I can say anything else, my phone buzzes.

"Seriously, who are you texting?"

"No one."

He glares my way, and I hold my phone a little tighter.

"You're obviously texting someone. Just tell me who it is."

"Why are you getting so mad? I'm just texting a friend."

He shoots me another nasty look before he darts his hand out to snatch the phone away from me, but I'm too quick, and I pull it away before he can grab it.

"Give me your phone," he demands on a low, steady tone, raising the hairs on my neck.

This isn't the first time he's spoken to me this way, and it makes me nervous. But what makes me even more nervous is what he'll do when he finds out that I'm texting Trent.

"I'm not giving you my phone."

His hands grip the steering wheel tighter as we drive south down I-95.

"Give me the goddamn phone, Kate."

"No."

When his eyes glaze over in rage, fear rushes into me. His

knuckles turn white, and at this point, I attempt to calm him down.

"Baby, relax. I'm here with *you*."

"You're not," he barks. "You're on your phone, giving someone else your attention, and your secrecy is pissing me off. I don't understand you, Kate. Here I am, giving you a great night, but it isn't enough, is it?"

He's being ridiculous.

"Of course it is."

My phone buzzes again, and my heart triple beats when he jerks the steering wheel and pulls off onto the shoulder of the interstate before throwing the car in park. A stream of icy cold panic swims through my veins.

"Give me that phone or else I'll pry it out of your fucking fingers."

"Caleb, stop! You're scaring me!"

Thrusting his hand across the console, he grabs ahold of my wrist and twists, sending a biting pain up my forearm and down my fingers.

"You're hurting me!" I wail as I hiss against his unyielding force.

"Give me the phone!"

He uses his other hand to rip my fingers away, and when I try to wrench my wrist out of his vise grip, he twists it even harder. I screech out against the excruciating pain and then give up. He snatches the phone away, and I burst into tears, cradling my throbbing hand against my chest. I want to yell and scream at him, but it'll only enrage him more, so I stare out the window and cry as he snoops through my phone. Everything inside me is pleading to get out of this car, but we're sitting on the side of the interstate at eleven o'clock at night. I'm trapped here with him, heartbroken and silently bawling in agony.

"Why the fuck are you telling Trent that you miss him? What the hell is going on between you two?"

THE secrets WE HELD

"Nothing," I manage to blubber through my tears.

"Don't lie to me," he says, but it sounds more like a threat.

"I'm not lying. He's just a friend."

"Bullshit!" he shouts, throwing the phone at me so hard it strikes my collarbone and tumbles to the floorboard, but I don't dare reach for it. Instead, I stare at him in sheer horror.

"I am not lying. Go ahead, look through the phone. See for yourself that I haven't talked to him in months."

"Have you fucked him?"

"What? God, no!"

"Then why are you telling him you miss him."

"Because he's a friend!" I blurt hysterically. "That's all. Just a friend."

He huffs, fuming in anger as he stares out the windshield. Breathing heavily in and out of his nose, his hands shake and he grits out, "If he is just a friend, why lie to me about it?"

I open my mouth but choke on every word that comes to me, too worried it'll be the wrong one. Eventually, I go with the only surefire thing I can possibly offer to diffuse him. "If you don't want me talking to him, just say the word, and I won't."

His teeth grind, and slowly, he turns to me, but his eyes no longer hold fury—they're sad. Almost lost. "You're the only thing that matters to me."

His pupils are dilated, and as I look into them, I see a tenderness within him that his temper defies. We sit in silence for a while as cars fly by, but time allows my mind to drift away from him and focus on the pain in my hand that's swelling up. The throbbing agony worsens when I bend my wrist and move my fingers to make sure he didn't break or fracture anything.

When I lift my head, I find his eyes fixed on my injured hand as I cradle it against my chest. "You hurt me."

"I'm so sorry." His words come on a breath laced in remorse, and if I felt any hatred toward him, it's masked by the compassion he's able to evoke in me. Gently, he takes my hand and brings it toward him, his thumb running along my puffy wrist that's beginning to unveil a bruise. "You have to know that I love you."

A tear rolls down my cheek. "Then why do you do this?" I ask, needing for him to clear this cloud of confusion around us.

"If I didn't care about you, I wouldn't get this upset." He kisses my knuckles tenderly. "You think I like doing this to you?" His expression fills with pain. "It kills me to know I hurt you, but if I were a man who didn't love you, I would just walk away because you wouldn't be worth everything you put me through. But I'm here when anyone else would've given up on you."

When I see his eyes rim in tears, my heart softens.

"I won't ever give up on you, Kate," he affirms, his voice cracking beneath the suffering I'm causing him.

Guilt combusts inside me, making me question why I was even texting Trent, knowing it would upset Caleb. He has insecurities and issues that he's made me well-aware of—Trent being one of them—yet, I continue to ignore them. I should be putting him first, but tonight, I pushed him aside and put the one guy he can't stand in front of him. I had no business doing that when Caleb is the one I love, he's the one sitting here now with tears running down his face because of the remorse he feels for hurting me because I hurt *him*.

"I don't think you understand how much I love you. How much I want to give you."

Running my fingers along his cheek, I wipe away his tears. "I feel the same way," I tell him. "I've never loved anyone as much as I love you; you have to believe me."

"It's hard to trust when I've been burned in the past."

"I know, and I'll be better, I promise. But I'm not your past,

Caleb." I unfasten my seatbelt and lean in toward him. "I'm here, and I'm not going anywhere. You don't have anything to worry about. But I don't like it when you get this angry and hurt me."

"I know. I'm sorry."

"It can't happen again."

He takes my face in his hands, affirming, "It won't. I promise." He folds his arms around me and holds me against him. "I won't ever hurt you again."

Even though he admits that his temper comes from a place of love, it doesn't make it right, and I don't want to have to face his violence again, but that doesn't erase the guilt I feel, knowing it was all my fault that this even happened.

"I'm so sorry I upset you," I tell him, adding, "I won't talk to Trent anymore."

He pulls back and rests his forehead against mine, and even though my wrist is still radiating in pain, it has nothing on the ache my heart is enduring. I only wish I could take back my behavior tonight so that none of this had to happen. All I can do is move forward and be better and love harder because it's the least I can give him when he's already given me so much.

Twenty

KATE

S ITTING OUT ON MY BALCONY, I KICK MY FEET UP ONTO THE RAILING and soak in the heat of the sun, thankful for the decline in humidity.

"I used to be obsessed with pigs when I was little," Ady says, kicking her feet up next to mine as she leans back in the patio chair. "For three years straight, I dressed up as a pretty pink piglet for Halloween."

I smile at my friend. "I bet you were adorable."

She flicks her hair as if she were a diva. "You know it."

Even though Ady and I see each other on campus, it's been months since we've spent time together like this. Having her at my condo presents a weird juxtaposition. On one hand, I'm happy to be in her company because I consider her a true friend. But, on the other hand, I'm so sad to have her here because it only magnifies how distant we've become.

It even extends beyond that because, ever since Caleb came into my life, I've shifted my stance with all my friends. Again, on one hand, it makes me sad to have my friendships suffering, but on the other, I'm so happy with Caleb.

"Are you going to Brody's Halloween party tonight?"

I close my eyes when a small gust of wind carries through my hair. "No. Caleb is coming over later, and we're just going to lie low."

"I thought for sure you'd be there, wearing something sexy."

"Sexy?"

"I could see you as a cat. A naughty cat in a black latex suit," she says with an equally naughty smirk.

"Oh my god! You're crazy."

We both laugh.

I was actually looking forward to dressing up this year and hitting Brody's party until he told me that Trent would be there. I've held true to my word with Caleb. Ever since the night of the gala, I haven't spoken to or texted Trent because I want to put Caleb's feelings first, something I don't think many people have done for him.

At first, I felt bad about severing my friendship with Trent because I like him and we had become good friends. Caleb then pointed out how Trent, in a backhanded way, was putting me down by putting down our relationship. I couldn't see it at first, but the more I thought about it, the more I understood where Caleb was coming from.

"Maybe next year," I tell her. "I might even buy a whip."

"No maybe about it. You better make it happen."

"What about you and Micah? What are you two doing tonight?"

"Camping out in his bed and watching TV. There's a *Nightmare on Elm Street* marathon on."

"How romantic," I deadpan.

"How lame are we?"

"We aren't lame, we're just in relationships."

She turns her head and looks out over the sky, seemingly in thought before asking, "So, how are things with you and Caleb?"

"They're good."

When her eyes meet mine, she looks skeptical. "Yeah?"

"Yeah," I assure. "Why are you asking?"

She shrugs and moves her focus back to the sky. "It's just . . ."

"Say it."

Dropping her feet from the railing, she sits up and responds, "Trent told me about what happened at the beach last month."

She brings to life a fluttering of anxious jitters when she mentions this. "What did he say?"

"That he didn't feel like things were quite right between you and Caleb."

What she doesn't say is that he told her that he saw Caleb grab me a little too roughly. Trent isn't the type of person to hold something like that back. Only, it wasn't as if Caleb meant to hurt me. He isn't an asshole.

"Trent has a thing against Caleb, you know that," I slough off with a shake of my head.

"I know," she says before adding, "He isn't the only one who has said something like that though."

"What is this all about?"

"Nothing." Her voice pitches with a hint of defensiveness, and she catches herself. "I just want to make sure you're all right."

"Why would you even think that I wouldn't be?"

"Because people talk."

"What people?" I ask, my annoyance blooming with how my relationship is being scrutinized, not only by Trent but also by Ady.

"Just people."

"What are they saying?"

She hesitates to answer.

"Just tell me."

Looking at me straight on, she comes out with it. "People are saying he hurts you. That they've seen you two fighting. That you're probably hiding bruises."

My jaw falls. "What? Are you serious?"

"Trent said he saw him grab you."

"Trent doesn't know what he saw," I defend.

"Brody said something similar as well."

"So, everyone is talking behind my back and spreading these rumors? Nice."

"Kate, these are your friends."

"Doesn't sound like it to me," I tell her before standing and walking back inside the condo.

"I'm not trying to fight," she says as she follows me. "But I care about you, and I would be a horrible friend if I didn't at least ask you about it, right? If something were going on, and I ignored it . . ."

"If you cared about me, you wouldn't be accusing Caleb, in a roundabout way, of hurting me. I mean . . . you know how people like to gossip. Do you know what this could do to his reputation?"

"I'm not worried about his reputation. I'm worried about *you.*"

"Well, don't be," I state and then take a seat on the couch. "People will always have their opinions, but I'm the one in the relationship, not them."

Even though he has put his hands on me, I know it wasn't because he meant to. He has a problem with his temper, but he's promised me that it won't happen again, and I trust him. It isn't worth betraying his trust to confide in her about this. I would never do that. He's so ashamed of his behavior, and at the same time, I'm ashamed too—embarrassed that she might think less of me if I told her this has happened and I'm still with him because, no matter what I would say, I doubt she would understand.

"Caleb is a great guy. He would never, and I mean *never,*

do anything to hurt me," I tell her adamantly. "Do we sometimes get into disagreements? Sure. But every couple does. That doesn't make him a bad person."

She stares at me with reluctance, and I hate that people are painting Caleb as a monster when it is so far from the truth.

"If you knew him, you would see how sweet and kind he is. He's good to me and so thoughtful. But I don't like having to defend my relationship to everyone."

"It's coming from a place of love."

"Is it? Because it feels like it's just fodder you all are feeding on."

"Maybe it is just fodder," she responds. "But if you heard those things about me, I would expect you to say something about it."

With a huff, I sink back into the couch.

"Trust me when I tell you that I'm not going around gossiping about you. Neither is Trent. None of us are. We're just concerned because on top of that, I feel like he's isolating you from all your friends."

I groan, rolling my eyes before sitting up again. "No one is isolating me. You're here right now, aren't you?"

"Right now, but this is the first time we've hung out in *months* when we used to hang out all the time."

"You can thank Trent for that," I tell her. "It's just hard because you live with him, so I don't feel like I can come over and chill with you anymore."

"But what about you never answering my calls or responding to my texts?"

"I'm sorry. I admit it; I've been a shitty friend, but that doesn't equate to Caleb holding me hostage." I take a moment to better compose myself before going on to add, "Look, Caleb isn't like us. He comes from a completely different world, and he doesn't really fit in with our crowd. I haven't been coming around much because I don't want him to feel uncomfortable."

She nods, and I can only hope she understands where I'm coming from.

"I could almost make the same accusation about you and Micah."

"What do you mean?"

"When I first met Micah when we were freshman, he always used to party. But now that he's dating you, he doesn't do that anymore. And I know it's because you aren't into that scene and Micah respects that, but someone could easily paint that as you being too controlling."

She takes a moment to think about what I just said. I wish, instead of her doubting me, she would just be happy for me.

"Trust me," I say. "I'm not the type of girl who would ever put up with a guy who was an asshole to me."

"Okay," she concedes softly. "I trust you."

"Are we cool then?"

She gives me a subtle nod.

"You want to get out of here?" I suggest, needing to cut the tension somehow. "I could use an iced coffee from that place that just opened down the street."

"Should we walk?"

"Yeah."

After we grab our phones and slip on our flip-flops, she stops me short of the door. "You're one of my closest friends," she tells me sincerely. "I just want you to know that I love you."

"I love you, too," I respond before we hug it out.

We then head down to the street and walk a couple of blocks over to grab our drinks. She doesn't bring up my relationship with Caleb again, and I couldn't be more thankful. There's nothing worse than having to defend yourself to the people who should trust you and have your back.

When she decides to head out, I try to let our earlier conversation go, but it's proving to be difficult. It's the knowing that everyone is talking about me and Caleb behind my back. Honestly, it's embarrassing. The last thing I want is for people to think I'm some weak, stupid girl who's in an unhealthy relationship.

I'm not blind to the fact that there are parts of our relationship that bother me. Do I like it when he yells at me and loses his temper? No. But he's only human, and I'm not some innocent bystander either. I'm well aware that I do things that set him off. I'm sure I would've lost my cool too if we were on a date and he was texting some girl. I can totally understand his issue with my friendship with Trent but that, in no way, makes him a bad person.

We all have our hang-ups, but Caleb is working on trying not to get so angry when something bothers him, which shows just how much he loves me. The areas of our relationship I'm not exactly proud of don't take away from the fact that we make each other happy.

And when he comes over to my place later in the evening, I wish they could all see the man I see. The one who shows up with a plastic pumpkin filled with all the best Halloween candy and a copy of my favorite horror flick.

"I figured we could camp out tonight," he says, and we do just that.

Grabbing a bunch of blankets and pillows, we make a huge pallet in the living room where we lie down, watch the movie, and over-indulge on candy. Nestled in his arms, I plant kisses along his jaw, and when he slips deeper down under the covers, meeting me eye to eye, I know everyone has him pegged all wrong.

He threads his fingers through my hair with a soft, "God, I love you so much."

Twenty-One

KATE

GATHERING THE HEM OF MY SHIRT, I ROLL IT UP TO EXPOSE THE splotchy, faded green and yellow bruises. I see the marks in the reflection of the mirror and want to believe they are independent of me, that they belong to someone else. Instead, they stare back at me, proving themselves to be real. In the moment when Caleb pinned me down so hard that he left bruises, there was no denying the reality.

So why, as I stand here now, does it feel so *unreal*?

As if the girl in the mirror is merely a fictional version of me.

I press the marred skin just above my right hipbone and wince through the pain that's still buried underneath.

I feel it.

Yet, I don't.

I'm me.

Yet, I'm not.

The man who did this should be a monster.

Yet, he isn't.

I forget what even sparked our fight because it got torn into a million different pieces that took the argument into a million different directions, all of which landed me at the mercy of his rage. It was the first time Caleb struck me. I've grown used to the screaming, the grabbing, and the shoving, but this time he *hit* me. I couldn't even comprehend what had happened after he backhanded me because in the very next second, he was on top of me, forcing me down as I kicked and screamed beneath him.

Eventually, I gave up and went lax. When he crawled off, he stormed out of my apartment, leaving me alone and in a state of shock.

I felt like crying, but no tears came.

I felt like running for help, but I told no one.

I felt like I hated him, but I loved him too much.

He came by the following day as I was leaving for campus. Still angry with him for breaking his promise that he made after our last fight, I didn't want to let him in. So, he stood outside of my door, upset and in so much torment for what he had done. The agony in his voice as he pleaded for my forgiveness was torture on my heart. Yes, he hurt me worse than what he had before after he swore he wouldn't, but that doesn't make my love for him just disappear.

"I can't lose you, Kate. Please," he urged. *"I love you. Please, let me in."*

I couldn't ignore him when he sounded so desperate, so I let him in and skipped my classes that afternoon.

"I fucked up," he admitted with his head in his hands as we sat on my couch.

In a way, it hurt worse hearing the pain he felt for what he had done than actually enduring it. My heart broke as he begged for my forgiveness, and while a tiny part of me didn't want to give it to him, a bigger part of me did.

It wasn't just him that held regrets. I played a part in igniting his fury, and I admitted my fault, telling him, *"I shouldn't have provoked you the way I did. I knew I was wrong, but I did it anyway."*

The two of us held each other, making promises to turn a

new leaf in our relationship and focus on each other more than what we had been. It was a few days later that I took a huge step and invited him to come home with me for Thanksgiving despite my having hesitations. The last thing I want is for my parents to catch wind of any of our issues.

Today is the day though.

Earlier this week, I drove back here to West Palm Beach to spend the holiday break with my family. Caleb is driving up today for Thanksgiving dinner tonight and staying through tomorrow. My mother already adores him even though they've yet to meet. She even suggested that Caleb could stay the night in one of the guest bedrooms, but I never told him that. Fear has found a way to embed itself inside me, and no matter how good Caleb and I are doing, it's something I can't shake. I walk upon eggshells most hours of most days, so I lied and told him that he would have to stay at a hotel.

When my sister barges into my bathroom, I shove my top down. "Can you knock?"

"Mom wants your help in the kitchen."

After shutting off the lights, I follow Audrina downstairs, where the aroma of freshly baked pumpkin pie fills my nose.

"Oh, man, that smells good." I moan as I walk over to the pie that's sitting on the counter.

"Get away from that," my mother playfully scolds while I'm bending over and taking a deep breath in. She then swats my butt with a dishtowel.

I jump and grab my ass. "Ouch!"

She laughs along with my sister.

"Where's Dad?"

"Pulling down the Christmas lights," my mother tells me as she hands me a sack of potatoes. "He decided to use your boyfriend for manual labor while he's here."

"And you think that's a good idea?"

"Why wouldn't it be?"

"Oh, I don't know," I say sarcastically. "What could possibly go wrong with Dad on the roof with a staple gun and my boyfriend?"

My mother shakes her head and smiles. "I think his intention is to spend some alone time with Caleb to get to know him, not to torture the guy with a staple gun."

"Choose your poison," my sister chimes in. "Staple gun or his pistol?"

"Neither."

My mom hands me the potato peeler. "It's your father. You already know it's going to be one or the other."

The three of us continue to chat while we prep the food. With the Thanksgiving parade playing on the television in the living room and the house filled with so much laughter, we barely hear the doorbell ring.

The moment I see my mother's beaming smile, I hold my hand up and stop her. "I'll get it. I don't want you bombarding him."

She pretends to act offended as I wipe my hands on a dishtowel before making my way to the front door.

"Hey, babe," he greets as I open the door, and then he pulls me in for a hug.

I hang on to him longer than he expects, and he senses my nerves. "You're worrying over nothing. Your parents are going to love me." As if to punctuate that fact, he leans back and shows me the bottle of wine he brought with him.

"You must be Caleb," my mother says as I lead him inside.

"Yes, ma'am." He smiles as he walks over to her.

After he kisses her cheek, he hands her the wine.

"Oh, that's so kind of you."

He sees my sister, who can't even hide her gawking smile. "Audrina, right?"

She nods, and as he's giving her a hug, she shoots me a thumbs-up, to which I roll my eyes.

My mother is still grinning as she says, "Can I get you something to drink?"

As they walk into the kitchen, Audrina and I trail slowly behind them.

"Oh my god, is that his car?" she whispers as she peers out the window.

I nod.

She slugs me in my arm. "You lucky skank!"

"Aren't you still seeing Zach?"

"Yeah, so?"

I laugh, and when we make it to the kitchen, I find Caleb standing over the sink, peeling a potato.

"Mom, Caleb didn't drive all the way here to work in the kitchen."

"He offered," she defends.

Caleb smiles. "It's fine. I'm happy to help."

I grab a cutting board and knife before sidling up next to him at the sink. As he peels, I chop.

"So, Caleb, Kate tells me you grew up in Chicago. What was that like?"

Caleb goes on to explain how great it was as a kid growing up in a big city—all lies to spare her the unimpressive truth. I listen to the two of them go back and forth with little effort, and I'm relieved to see how easily they're getting along. Not that I should've had any concerns. Caleb is a natural charmer. It's what immediately drew me to him.

"Everything is down," my father calls out when he comes in from the garage.

"Caleb is here," my mother announces, and my father's annoyed grunt reaches us before he enters the kitchen. It's all part of the game he likes to play when my sister and I bring a boy around.

"Caleb," my dad greets, holding his hand out for Caleb to shake.

"Good to meet you, sir."

"Call me Officer Murphy."

"Don't call him that," I chime in as I step next to Caleb. "His name is Steve."

Caleb wears an uncertain smile until my mother playfully swats my dad on the arm, and then he relaxes.

Dad ignores us girls, keeping his focus on Caleb. "How old are you?"

"Twenty-two, sir."

He nods. "Grab a couple of beers from the fridge and meet me in the garage."

When my father steps out of the room, Caleb gives me a questioning look, and I tell him, "Don't worry. He just wants your help with the Christmas lights."

He then grabs the beers and makes his way outside.

"Are you worried?"

I hand my sister the peeler. "No. Caleb is a solid guy. I'm sure Dad will like him."

Once the potatoes are prepped and mashed, Audrina and I start working on the stuffing while Mom tends to the turkey and watches over the cranberries that are on the stove. One by one, we pull each dish together, and when my sister puts the rolls into the oven to warm up, I go outside to check on the guys.

Only, when I look around, I see my father and not my boyfriend. "Where's Caleb?"

"Back here," he shouts as he juts up his hand from behind

one of the eaves while my dad casually sits on the roof and sips his beer.

I shoot him an admonishing glare. "Dad."

He just smiles and takes another swig.

"Dinner is almost ready."

"Good. I'm starved."

"Me too," Caleb says when he shuffles into view.

"What happened to your shirt?" I ask when I realize he's no longer in his button-up.

"I didn't want to get it dirty. I had some clean clothes in my gym bag I keep in my car."

"Are you done with him, Dad?"

He claps Caleb on the shoulder. "I appreciate your help."

"No problem."

"And Kate's right," he tells him. "You can call me Steve."

And with that small gesture, I know Caleb has won him over.

When the two of them are down from the roof, I show Caleb up to my room so he can freshen up.

"So, what did you two talk about?" I ask as he washes his hands in my bathroom.

"What you would expect," he says. "My family, school, hobbies. Nothing too intense."

He walks back into the room, and I hand him his shirt.

"He didn't give you the third degree, did he?"

"More like the tenth degree," he chuckles. "Nothing I couldn't handle."

When we make it back downstairs, the formal table is set and all the food is laid out in a mouth-watering spread.

After we take our seats, my mom, my dad, my sister, and I start to look between each other, and after a few seconds of silence, the four of us bust out laughing.

Caleb eyes me. "Am I missing something here?"

"Grace."

"Who's saying it this year?" my sister asks.

My mother then tells Caleb, "We aren't a very religious family, but it always feels wrong to eat without saying grace during the holidays."

"Mom is afraid God will strike her with lightning," I joke.

"I'm happy to say grace," Caleb offers, stunning not only me but also the rest of my family.

Mom smiles, and when we bow our heads, Caleb gives a very thoughtful blessing, erasing any worry I had about bringing him home.

"Caleb," my mother starts as she cuts a bite of turkey. "When do you graduate?"

"Next semester in May."

"Will you be staying in Miami?"

As he pierces his fork into his green beans, he says, "Honestly, I haven't made up my mind just yet."

That catches me off guard because he's never mentioned not knowing if he was going to stay in Miami. "Where would you go if you don't stay?" I ask, but I already know the answer.

"Nowhere in particular. I'm just keeping my options open."

He says this, but there's no question he would go back home to Chicago. Nothing else makes much sense.

Once my parents move on to another subject, he leans a bit closer to me and murmurs, "You have no reason to worry. We'll talk about it another day."

I force a smile and nod because he's right. This isn't the time to discuss his future and how I fit in to it.

After everyone is stuffed and tossing their napkins onto the table, I help my mother clear the dishes while my dad tells Caleb stories about his time on the SWAT team. The two go back and forth, and after I make another trip into the kitchen, my mother tugs my arm and pulls me in for a hug.

"What's this all about?"

Drawing back, she keeps her hands on my shoulders. "I'm just really happy for you. Caleb is . . . well, he's nothing like the boys you've liked in the past."

"Is that a good thing?"

"You have no idea. I mean, Caleb is so polite and respectful. The way he looks at you . . ." She drifts off with a smile.

Hearing what my mother has to say and watching how easily my father tossed aside his game of intimidation with Caleb settles the hesitations I sometimes feel about him. Surely, if he was a bad person, their parental spidey senses would know it, right? I need to let go of the idea that couples are always perfect and that relationships don't come with flaws. But the flaws we do have hold no sway over on the foundation of love our relationship stands on.

When all that is left of dessert is a few crumbs and the sun has set, my mother sips her decaf coffee while flipping through the Black Friday ads and my father retires to the couch to watch football. With everyone doing their own thing, Caleb and I go to my room for some much-needed alone time.

I rest my head on Caleb's chest as we lie on my bed. We don't say much as we soak in the quietness of the room, the only sounds coming from the football game downstairs.

"I think I ate too much," he eventually murmurs, and I let go of a breathy giggle.

"Me too. But I'm not going to lie, I would still force down a second piece of pie."

"Same. Your mother is an amazing cook." He plants a kiss on top of my head. "When do you want to head to the hotel?"

"What do you mean?"

"You look like you can barely keep your eyes open."

Slowly, I sit up, and he follows suit. "Oh, I was planning to stay the night here. I thought you knew that."

"What do you mean you're staying here?"

"Exactly that. There's no way my father would be cool with us sharing a hotel room," I tell him as I watch frustration brimming in his eyes.

"But it was fine when you came to Chicago."

With a guilty grin, I admit, "I lied to him about that. I told him you were staying with your parents."

Caleb huffs in annoyance.

"I'm sorry, but he's super protective, and I don't want to outright disrespect him."

"But you'll outright disrespect me?"

I shift to sit on my knees so that I'm facing him. "That's not it at all."

"I gave up spending Thanksgiving with my family to be here with you, and now you're making me go back to the hotel by myself? You're being selfish."

"I'm not being selfish," I defend, trying to keep my voice down.

When he gets off the bed, I already know he's getting himself riled up, and I go into a silent panic, praying he doesn't raise his voice or do anything that would draw attention to us.

He paces a few steps away, and I walk over to him. "If I had it my way, I would go with you, trust me. But he's my father, and I respect him."

In an instant, he snaps.

He grabs my upper arms and seethes, "So I'm just shit to you? My feelings don't matter?"

"Of course they matter," I say as I try to twist out of his hold, but he doesn't relent. I hiss as his fingers dig into the muscle, sending a stabbing pain down my arms and into my palms. "Let go," I quietly beg, worried he's going to put more bruises on me.

"I do so much for you, and I don't even know why because all you do is think about yourself."

When the black in his eyes widen, my fear catapults. Only, instead of begging and sobbing, I get angry. "Let go."

He squeezes tighter, forcing my knees to give.

"My father is downstairs." I fume under my breath. "Let go. Now."

With that, he does. When his hands drop away, I take a few steps back as my arms throb in succession with my pulse.

I stare at him, wondering what he's going to do next. He stands for a moment before opening his mouth and telling me, "I fucking hate that you're constantly testing my love for you. It's like you get off on pissing me off."

"You know that's not true."

"Then tell me what is true."

I could snap and be defiant the way my bones are aching to do—it's what I should do. Yet, it would only set him off again.

So, for the moment, I let go of my own feelings of anger toward him to see past the hostility in his eyes, straight through to the man I know he wants to be, the man who's strong enough to temper his emotions and not let them take control over him.

I stride over to him, cup my hands along his scruffy jaw, and kiss him. I don't even care that he won't kiss me back, I keep my lips locked to his while tears well in my eyes.

When I draw back and look up into his eyes, I see how badly he craves to simply be loved.

"You're my world," I give him. "And it breaks my heart when you question my love for you because it's boundless. I wish you could see that. I wish you could crawl inside my heart and feel what I feel because you would never have to question me again. My staying here to keep my parents happy has noth-ing to do with how much I love you. It has everything to do with how much I want them to love you too."

As I say this, he softens, relaxing his tense muscles. Remorse glosses over his eyes before his head drops to mine with a lamenting, "I'm so sorry."

I sling my arms around his neck and hold him tightly, hating that I bring out these painful emotions in him, but more than anything I'm happy. Happy that we didn't fall into another sit-uation we would both wind up regretting. It's a victory in my book, and it gives me hope that we have the ability to move past the dysfunctional toxicity we've been fighting to overcome.

"You have nothing to be sorry for," I assure.

Twenty-Two

KATE

"SO, WHAT WAS IT LIKE GETTING BOTH FAMILIES TOGETHER FOR Thanksgiving?" I ask Ady.

It's been six months since I was at her place, and when she invited me over, I was reluctant. The promise I made to stay away from Trent was one I didn't want to break. But Ady assured me he was out with buddies, so I came.

"It wasn't that big of a deal because my mom already knows Micah's parents, but it was fun getting everyone together."

"Seems serious."

She shakes off my comment, saying, "It only seems that way because we've been close friends for so long. Like I said before, Micah and I are taking things slow."

I smirk. "But you're in his bed every night, right?"

She grabs a pillow and flings it at my head.

"You're such a pervert."

"Whatever," I say with a shrug.

"How did it go with Caleb meeting your family? Did your dad embarrass you?"

"I felt like it went well, and no, my dad seemed to like him, so it all worked out."

"And what about you? How are the two of you doing?"

"Amazing. Seriously, Ady, he's everything I could ever want in a boyfriend."

I ignore the crooked look she's giving me. It's old news that she, along with others, doesn't particularly like Caleb.

When she sees I'm not going to respond to her look, she moves past it. "So, what are your plans for Christmas?"

"I don't really know. We talked about me going with him to Chicago, but I know my parents would be upset if I didn't go home and spend the holiday with them. I'm just trying to figure out the best plan."

The front door slams, catching my attention, and when I hear Trent's hostile voice, I clam up. I can't make out what he's saying, but whatever it is, it isn't kind.

"I thought you said he wasn't going to be here."

"He wasn't supposed to be," she responds as if it's no big deal. "I still don't understand why you can't be friends with him."

"You make it sound like it isn't my choice."

"Is it?" she questions suspiciously.

"Yes," I stress. "From the very start, he's disrespected my relationship with Caleb."

Her brow quirks slightly, a reaction I doubt she's aware of but one that exposes her doubt. "It's just sad. We all used to have so much fun together."

"Yeah, we did," I agree.

"What about the New Year's Eve party Brody has been talking about throwing?"

"Don't give me a hard time about parties when you haven't gone to a single one since I've met you."

She laughs because she knows it true.

"Trent told me how much you all would party in high school, so I don't get what your hang up is."

"Nothing. I guess I'm just not into it anymore."

"Lame," I tease at the same time my phone chimes with a text.

> Caleb: Getting out of class in 20 minutes. Want to meet me on campus during my break?
> Me: Yeah. I'll text when I get there. I'll meet you on the steps at the lake by the student center.
> Caleb: See you then.

Tucking my phone away, I tell Ady, "I need to get going."

"Everything all right?"

"Yeah," I say as I stand. "Caleb is about to get out of class and he wants to hang out before his next one starts."

"Okay." Ady hops off the bed and gives me a hug. "Thanks for coming over."

"We'll get together again soon. I promise."

"Yeah, yeah," she jokes, waving her hand dismissively.

"See ya."

When I head out of her room, I stop and wonder if Trent's door is open. I can't tell, and I can't see into the living room to see if he's in there. I really don't want to run into him and have to explain why I've cut him completely out of my life. The last time we spoke was through those text messages the night of the gala almost three months ago. I didn't bother contacting him after that to tell him that I wouldn't be talking to him any longer. Honestly, I don't want to have that conversation at all, so I simply avoid it altogether.

But now, as I walk past his room, I see him sitting on the edge of his bed with his cell phone dangling from his fingers. His head is down, and he looks in my direction as I pass, our eyes meeting for a mere split second. When I hit the living room, something unexplainable stops me from opening the front door and leaving. Instead, I hesitate. Standing in the middle of the room, I contemplate whether I should follow what my head is telling me to do or if I should listen to my heart.

Finally, I turn on my heel and walk back to his room because I can't ignore the tug he has on me—the same tug he's always had. Nervous, since I've put so much distance between us, I knock softly on his open door, and when he looks up, he's expressionless.

Silence spans between us until I give a timid, "Hey."

"What are you doing here?"

I take a step inside the room. "I came to see Ady."

He nods and tosses his phone onto his nightstand. "You should probably go before Caleb finds out you were talking to me."

A tiny part of me is ashamed that he's calling me out on it—no, I feel this way because *I* did it. I should at least be able to own that choice enough to admit it to myself.

"I'm sorry I bailed, I—"

"You didn't bail, you fucking vanished. But whatever, you know."

"Don't do that," I say, taking a seat next to him.

His eyes stay downcast as we sit with no words spoken. His hair has gotten longer since the last time I saw him. I want to give him a hard time, make a joke, but every word that comes to me feels wrong.

After a while, without lifting his head to look at me, he says, "I'm worried about you."

"Look at me." It takes a second, but eventually, he meets my eyes. "I need you to trust me when I tell you that you have it all wrong. There is no reason for you to worry about me at all. I'm not sure how Caleb has gotten a bad rap with you, but he's a good man; He loves me."

"It doesn't erase what I saw that day at the beach."

I want to deny that he saw anything, but I let it go because the last thing I want to do is get into another argument with him over nonsense. Instead, I give myself a moment, and when he looks at me again, I say the first thing I feel.

"I miss you."

Before he can say anything, his phone starts ringing. He picks it up, reads the name of the person who's calling, and drops the phone back down.

He appears aggravated, so I ask, "Who was that?"

"No one."

I let out an exasperated sigh. "Can we just talk without all this animosity or whatever this is between us?"

"Sorry, I'm just having a shitty day."

"Want to talk about it?"

"Nothing to really talk about," he responds, closing down, but I don't want him to push me away.

"Is everything okay with your mom back home?"

As soon as I ask, he breathes heavily, kicking his legs onto the bed and reclining against his pillows.

"I'll take that as a no," I respond. "So, what's going on?"

"Same shit as always."

In the past, trying to get Trent to open up has been like pulling teeth, and even though I know I should leave and get over to campus, I can't bring myself to go just yet because I care about him.

"Are you just going to leave me guessing?" I half tease, but he doesn't crack a smile, which is way out of character. Whatever is weighing on him clearly has him in a mood.

"She's seeing someone else," he eventually reveals. "Her divorce hasn't even been finalized, and she already has the next guy lined up."

"How did you find this out?"

"She told me. She's always telling me shit I don't need to know or be involved in."

He stares at the ceiling before reaching over and grabbing his pen. After clicking a few times to turn it on, he takes a long hit and then holds it out for me. Having not done any pot for so long, I give in and welcome the calmness it brings when I take a pull and suck it down deep into my lungs. It's just enough to take the edge off, so I hand it back to him and watch as he takes a second hit.

"Does she always do this?"

He gives a humorless laugh. "She's working on husband number six, so what do you think?"

"I'm sorry."

"The woman can't be alone. I love her, but I'm getting to the point where I'm sick of being her fucking therapist all the time."

"Have you talked to her about how you feel?"

Again, another pissed off laugh sounds from under his breath. "If it weren't for me, she'd have no one looking out for her."

"What about your brother?"

"She doesn't talk to him like she does with me. I swear, I feel more like her friend than her son," he admits, exposing a layer that can't be easy for him. "I've always been the one protecting and watching out for her when it should've been the other way around." Tilting his chin up, he focuses his attention back up to the ceiling to avoid eye contact when he reveals, "I remember when I was a little kid, maybe in the second grade or somewhere around then, sitting in bed with her while she cried into her pillow after another dude walked out on her."

A tiny piece of my heart chips away, inflicting a sharp pang of sadness through me. He sits back up and swings his legs off the edge of the bed so he's sitting next to me again.

"I hate to say it because it makes me sound like a shitty person, but I'm tired of looking out for her. But, fuck, she's my mom."

"You don't sound shitty at all," I tell him, thinking twice before resting my hand on his leg that's touching mine. "Maybe you should talk to her about this though."

"I'm done talking about it altogether."

"Why do I get the feeling this is the first time you've talked about it at all?"

"One time too many."

"Why are you so quick to shut down?"

He turns and looks at me with a cocked brow. "Why do you care?"

"Because you're my friend?"

"Yeah? You treat all your friends like this?" he throws at me. "How many months has it been since I last saw you?"

"That isn't fair."

"Not that I give a shit. I mean . . . you do you, but don't come around and pretend like you care."

I want to tell him that he's to blame too. He's the one who kept on bashing Caleb after I told him to stop, but he didn't care enough about my feelings to do so—he just kept on. There are so many crappy comments he's made that I can point to as examples of how shitty of a friend he's been to me. I could throw all of that back at him and storm out of here, but I don't because I'm growing tired of us slinging insults at each other.

"I *do* care, Trent." I tug on his shoulder to get him to face me. "Hey," I say, needing him to hear me. "I really do care about you."

He takes another hit off his pen, and I can tell he's already stoned, so I give up.

"I should get going."

I stand and start walking out of his room before he stops me with, "Wait."

When I turn around, he gets off the bed and walks straight toward me, not stopping until he has me in his arms. I wish I knew all the thoughts in his head as I hug him back. I've never seen Trent act this way before, so I keep my arms banded around him, giving him the touch, the comfort, whatever it is he needs. And, in a way I'm not brave enough to admit, I need it too. I know I should be racing across town to get to Caleb, but I stay with my head pressed against Trent's chest as we hold on to each other.

"I miss you too," he eventually says.

Twenty-Three

KATE

A STORM IS BREWING OFFSHORE. BLANKETS OF DARK GRAY HANG above the water and slowly blow toward land. The shift in air pressure has really intensified the waves, so I grabbed my board and headed out here to clear my mind and get a little space. Space from everything and everyone—including myself.

Another semester is about to come to an end, Christmas is just around the corner, and it feels as if the walls are closing in on me. It's an indefinable cloud I'm walking through with so much confliction.

I saw Ady and Trent two weeks ago, and ever since, I've had a pit in my stomach. Somehow, I've managed to push everyone out of my life. Love has swept me away into an alternate world that revolves solely around Caleb. The man gives me so much that I want, but I'm starting to understand that it isn't without cost.

Bobbing over waves out here in the ocean on my board, I'm all alone.

I'm always alone, and it's starting to affect me in ways I keep hidden.

When I see a perfect swell heading in, I flip onto my stomach and begin to paddle. The rush of water propels me, and I pop up, dragging my fingertips along the lip of the break as it carries me for a decent ride. The wind whips through my hair as droplets of water spray against my skin, and I'm free. All my senses focus on this moment—the salt perfuming the air, the cold water pelting my flesh, the cool breeze rushing from all around.

Reaching the closeout, I hear a faraway, "Fuck yeah!" right before I kick out and sink down into the water. As I hang on to my board and float, I turn toward the shore and see Trent zipping up his wetsuit.

"What are you doing here?" I shout as he grabs his board and jogs out into the water.

While he paddles to where I am, I pull myself up and sit on my board. I came out to be alone, but I can't help being glad that he's here. I miss my friend I used to spend so much time with.

As he approaches, he raises his chest and sits up.

"What are you doing here?" I repeat now that he can hear me.

"Same thing you are. Surf report said there would be better than decent swells with the storm coming in. Didn't want to miss out," he tells me. "You here by yourself?"

"Yeah, Caleb is in class, and I was bored sitting at the condo."

"I hear ya. Micah's at campus too, and Ady got an itch in her panties to teach herself how to cook."

"How's that going?"

He grabs the edge of my board, pulls me closer, and ducks his head so he's almost pressed against me. "You smell that shit?"

I grab a handful of his now ear-length wet hair and take a deep whiff. "All I smell is ocean water."

He draws back. "Wolfgang Schmuck decided to toss some bacon into the oven and not set a timer. She burnt the living shit out of it," he complains. "Smoked out the whole condo and set off the alarm."

I laugh.

"Everything smelled like charred ass."

"Poor Ady."

"Fuck that. Poor *me*." He glances over my shoulder, kicks his legs to turn his board around, and starts paddling to catch the wave that's coming while he hollers back to me, "See you later, masturbator!"

I watch as he digs his hands into the water, pops up, and catches the wave, not realizing the huge smile on my face. He does a roundhouse kickback but he wipes out and jumps into the water.

My energy lifts as he paddles back to me with a sarcastic, "You gonna sit on your cinnamon ring all day like a slacker?"

Cutting the water with my hand, I splash him. "You are so gross!"

He laughs and whips his head back and forth a couple of times to shake out the water. "Come on, let's ride before the rain hits."

And with that, we paddle in different directions, parallel to the shore, so we don't have to fight over the waves. Even if we aren't talking, his presence out here changes the trajectory of my mood. Trent has a way about him, a calming ease that people around him feed off—including me. Vanished are my thoughts from earlier as I catch a killer ride while Trent yells nonsense at me and cheers me on.

Slowly, the clouds roll in, kicking up the wind before it starts to sprinkle. We wait as long as we can before we paddle in, and when we reach the shore, I ask, "Have you seen any lightning?"

With our boards tucked under our arms, we stand in the sand and look over the water.

"I don't see any," he says.

"Yeah, me neither."

Before we completely call it and head out, we take a minute to sit in the sand and watch the clouds as the sprinkles grow into heavier drops.

"That was fun," I tell him.

"Yeah, you gotta stop avoiding coming out here."

"I'm not avoiding."

He gives me an animated *yeah whatever* look, and I rock into him, nudging my shoulder into his.

"I'm serious," he states. "You've been steering clear of me for so long that you've given me a complex."

"You're far from having a complex."

"Tell me you haven't been avoiding me then."

But I can't, and he knows it.

"That's what I thought."

"Trent," I start and then stop. Although he wears a smirk, I know he wouldn't bring it up if it didn't bother him, and I hate that I'm the one who's deliberately acting this way, but I'm stuck between two guys who despise each other. I know he wants me to just own up and tell him the truth; a part of me wants that to, so I give him what I can to help take some of the blame off Caleb. "You're right."

He shifts his focus off the water and puts it on me.

"I *have* been avoiding you."

"Why?"

"Because . . ." I pause; it isn't easy to be straightforward with him. The two of us, we run around in circles with each other.

"Tell me."

"That night at your party . . . when you kissed me . . ." My eyes find their way to the crashing waves, and I keep them there when I continue. "It kind of got me thinking that maybe you were interested." I shake my head with a lifeless chuckle. "It was stupid to think that you would be, but it confused me. I didn't like not knowing where I stood with you, and I felt like a needed space."

It takes me a moment to get the courage to face him, and when I do, I'm met with a sympathetic expression. "I'm sorry. I thought we were just having fun."

I nod.

"It's not in me to want to lead people on or hurt them."

"I know that." I then give him a small smile, and he returns it. It's an unspoken acknowledgement of understanding.

He's the first to break the connection when he takes a U-turn, asking, "So, are you going to blow me off tonight?"

"Tonight?"

"The party at Zach's. Brody said you'd be there."

Shit.

Last I heard, Trent wasn't going at all, which is why I begged Caleb to go with me. He's been over all the parties for some time now, but he agreed to come to Zach's. I never would've pressed the issue as much as I did if I knew Trent was going to be there.

"You don't have to do what he tells you to."

"You think that's what I do?"

With utter confidence, he says, "I know it is."

"You're wrong," I defend, shaking my head.

"Yeah?"

I nod.

He then stands as the clouds completely split open and the rain comes pouring down. "Then prove it," is all he says before grabbing his board and jogging up the beach to his SUV, leaving me alone.

I linger, letting the rain fall on me as the ocean churns. Now that Trent has left, my mood returns, but it's heavier than it was before. I contemplate texting Caleb and making up some excuse as to why we should ditch the party, but I don't want to keep tiptoeing around the beef the two of them have with each other.

When I get back to my condo, I find Caleb studying at the bar in my kitchen. He's had a key to my place for a week now and doesn't hesitate to come over often.

"There you are," he says, looking up from his books.

I take a second to prop my surfboard against the wall and then walk over to give him a kiss.

"How was the beach?"

"Peaceful," I tell him as I head to my bathroom to toss my wetsuit over the shower rod. "How long have you been here?" I call out across the condo.

"Not long. About twenty minutes or so."

When he strolls into the bedroom, I tell him, "I'm going to jump in the shower. Give me a few."

But he surprises me after only a couple of minutes when he slips in with me. We spend a good amount of time under the steamy water, making love.

It's indescribable how happy he makes me in moments like this when he abandons all his stress so that we give ourselves to each other. I swear, it's the best feeling in the world. One I wouldn't trade for anything.

After a long nap, Caleb moves to the living room to order in dinner for us, and I take my time getting dressed. I end up in shorts, a strappy flowy top, and a pair of Chuck Taylors. Once I'm happy with how I look, I head out of my bedroom and find Caleb with a scowl on his face as he reads something on his phone.

"Everything okay?"

"Yeah, just reading my emails."

I walk into the kitchen and grab a bottle of water, and when Caleb stands from the couch, there's agitation written all over his face. He can lie and tell me everything is fine, but when he's upset, he wears it boldly.

"Hey," I say when he walks into the kitchen and takes the bottle from my hand before unscrewing the top and downing a few gulps. "I can tell there's something wrong."

"We can talk about it later."

I've heard this from him so many times that I have to force myself not to show my annoyance. For almost our whole relationship, I've been out of the loop, and I wish he would just let me in on what the heck he keeps trying to push off.

"What if I don't want to talk about it later?"

"Then we won't talk about it at all."

"That's not what I mean," I say, taking the bottle out of his hand and setting it on the countertop. "Let's talk about it now."

"I don't think now is a good time."

"I think it's a perfect time," I respond on the edge of firm. He stares at me as I wait for him to speak, but when he takes too long, I urge, "Just say it, Caleb."

"I'm moving back to Chicago after graduation."

And now it's me who can't speak because I'm too shocked to find words. All he has ever talked about was starting a new life for himself here in Miami, and now he's moving back to the very place I thought he was trying to get away from.

"What do you mean?" I ask because all my thoughts are nothing but a tornado in my head.

"I mean exactly what I said. I already have a job lined up."

"Are you kidding me? Why? Why would you go back? I thought your plan was to stay here . . . with me."

"It was, but . . ."

"But what?" I question as an emotion, lodged somewhere between angry and sad, punctures through my heart.

He turns and takes a few steps away from me, raking his hand through his hair.

"Talk to me!" I demand, my voice pitching.

"It isn't like I have much of a choice."

"Of course you have a choice." I walk over to where he stands and step in front of him. "I don't even need to ask if this has something to do with your father, do I?"

"You don't get it."

"No, I get it," I tell him. "What I don't get is why you're letting him control you when you're a grown man."

The muscles in his neck constrict with anger, but I'm mad too. Mad that he would make these plans and hide them from me.

"He threatened my trust fund."

"So what? Who cares?"

"I care!" he shouts.

"It's just money."

"Yeah, a *lot* of fucking money, Kate!" he snaps before pacing away again. "He's the trustee; he controls it all."

Raising my arms in defeat, I then drop them back to my sides. "So what? You're choosing money over me?"

He quickly turns back to me. "No. It's not that . . . it's complicated."

"Then un-complicate it."

"They're my parents, Kate. They're the only family I have, and even though their methods are entirely off, I need them in my life."

It's a stance I can't argue with because it's one I used with him over Thanksgiving. I just hate that they hold so much over his head, knowing he won't turn his back on them. It's so unfair.

When he faces me again, he seems to have calmed a bit. "I want you to come with me."

I swear my jaw hits the floor. "I can't."

"Don't you love me?"

"Why is it always about that, Caleb? Of course, I love you,

but I still have two years of college. This is my home. This is where all *my family* and friends are."

"There're schools in Illinois."

"Are you serious right now?" I screech, shocked that he isn't seeing this as a big deal like I am. Heck, he doesn't even seem to understand why I'm upset. Did he really think I would give up everything I've worked for to move to Chicago because his father threatened to take away his stupid trust fund?

"I don't want to lose you, Kate." His head drops, and I don't doubt that this has to be tearing him up on the inside. "I can't," he admits, his voice cracking.

"You won't," I assure before hugging him. I'm still angry that he is choosing to allow his parents to threaten him like this, that he's choosing money over me, and that he didn't talk to me about it before he made his choice. "We'll just . . . I don't know, but we'll figure it out."

We continue to hold each other, agreeing that we should drop it for now and enjoy tonight, promising that we'll talk about it more tomorrow.

My hand never leaves his as he drives across town to Zach's house. My heart droops low in my chest while I try not to think about what it would feel like to lose Caleb. It's the very last thing I want—to be without him—but I have no clue what the solution would be.

When we turn down the street Zach lives on, we find the road packed with cars lining the curb. Eventually, we find a spot a block away, and after he parks the car, he unfastens his seatbelt and turns to me.

"I need you to know that you are my world, and the only reason I didn't tell you sooner was because I was scared to. I was afraid of how you would react."

As I slide my hand along his jaw, I feel the confliction that's all around him. "I can understand that, but I need you to talk to me about this type of stuff, okay?"

"I know. You're right. I should've been upfront with you."

"And you're not going to lose me." I kiss him before adding, "I don't know what the answer is, but I love you, and we'll figure it out."

Twenty-Four

MUSIC PULSES AGAINST THE WALLS WHEN WE STEP INTO THE party. Caleb goes to find us drinks, and when I scope the room, I'm surprised to spot Micah. Immediately, I start looking for Ady. I expect her to be right next to him, which she isn't, so I make my way over to find out where she is.

"Hey, Kate," he greets, holding out his arm for a quick hug.

"Hey, yourself. Is Ady here?"

"You know better than to ask me that," he jokes.

"What is she doing tonight?"

"Her mom is in town for the weekend, so she's staying at the hotel with her."

When he jumps back in to conversation with his buddies, I look over my shoulder to see if Trent is around, nervous about him and Caleb crossing paths, but I come up empty.

"Hey, babe," Caleb says when he joins me, handing me a cup of beer.

I catch Micah's irritation when he glares at Caleb. I think it's safe to assume that Trent told him about Caleb putting his hands on me, but I shake it off. What else can I do?

We hang out and shoot the shit until a loud ruckus catches my attention. This time, when I peer over my shoulder, I see Trent smashing his beer bottle against some random girl's, and when it erupts like a volcano, they start chugging. I watch as the foam spills out the sides of Trent's mouth and onto the floor. The people around them cheer him and the girl on.

"You made it," Brody announces as he joins us, snapping my attention away from the scene across the room. "Dude, I'm feeling rejected," he says through a chuckle.

"What? Why?"

"You didn't tell me you and Trent were hitting the beach today. I would've come out with you guys."

Instantly, my insides go cold, and when I glance to Caleb, I feel the heat of his anger boiling. We haven't even been here thirty minutes, and now I have to put out this fire.

"I thought you were going by yourself?"

"I did," I tell Caleb. "I was about to pack up and leave and he just randomly showed up."

"How was it out there?" Brody asks.

"Pretty decent."

Brody, who is clearly unimpressed by my answers, turns his attention to Micah, and Caleb takes a step away from the group.

I follow him as he puts space between us and everyone else. "You lied to me," he accuses.

"No. I didn't lie. Like I said, as I was leaving he showed up."

"So, why didn't you tell me?"

"Because it wasn't a big deal."

He doesn't like it when I say that, and he grabs my wrist, pulling me through the room. When we hit the hallway, he opens the first door on our left, which leads to a small bedroom, and shoves me inside. The door slams behind us, muffling the music, and I jerk my wrist out of his hold.

"I thought I told you that I didn't want the two of you hanging out."

"Caleb, relax. I wasn't hanging out with him," I say, already

knowing that, even though this afternoon was completely innocent, he'll never see it that way. "Like I said, he showed up as I
was leaving."

"That isn't how Brody made it sound."

"Brody wasn't even there, so how would he know?"

He stares down at me as his chest rises and falls with halting,
shallow breaths while he battles his anger.

"I promise you, it wasn't a big deal."

He turns his back to me and takes a few steps away, curling
and uncurling his fists. It's the same thing he does every time he
loses his shit, and after our earlier conversation about Chicago, I
fear this is a recipe for disaster.

"Caleb, please—"

"You lied!"

"No, I didn't. I swear."

"I give you everything!" he shouts. "And, yet, you still feel
the need to sneak around with that piece of trash."

"He's not—" I immediately stop myself from defending
Trent, but Caleb doesn't let it go.

"He's not what?"

"Nothing."

With the look of the devil piercing through his eyes, he
stalks toward me. "Say it, Kate. He's not what?" he antagonizes,
goading me to finish my broken thought, but I don't because
I know better, and that only ticks him off more. "Fucking say
it!" He grabs me roughly by my arms, driving me backward and
slamming me into the wall with so much force that my head ric-
ochets against it, sending a splintering pain slicing through my
skull and momentarily blinding me.

"Caleb, stop!"

He clamps my arms even tighter, catapulting me beyond the
realm of panic.

"Why do you do this to me? You think you're fucking cute, whoring around and throwing it in my face?"

"Stop! You're hurting me!"

"And you don't think you're hurting me?" He yanks me forward and throws me back once more. My vision blurs on impact, and I want to cry for help, but I'm too terrified.

"Let me go!"

He grips my jaw so viciously that my teeth skin the inside of my cheek, causing my mouth to bleed. He's in a complete blackout rage at this point. His eyes darken while I jerk my body to try to get out of his hold, but he's unrelenting.

I've only seen him this furious a few times before, but after the last time, after he busted my lip open with his fist, he swore to me it would never happen again. Yet, here we are with him lost to whatever darkness lives inside him and with me getting treated like nothing more than a punching bag. I begin thrashing to get away, and in the very next second, the two of us are going at it, fighting against each other, but he's so much stronger than I am.

Still, the palm of my hand strikes beneath his chin, snapping his teeth into his tongue. He steps back in a moment of distraction.

I see the blood on his lips.

His eyes lift to mine, and my heart pounds with unimaginable violence when he lunges at me with his balled-up fist raised. He comes at me so fast that I can't get away before his knuckles hammer down into the crest of my cheek, snapping my head to the side so severely that my neck pinches in agonizing fire. The impact knocks me to the ground, sending the other side of my face into a small table. A lamp crashes on the floor next to me, shattering into slivers of porcelain and glass that cut into my arms as I scramble to get away from him.

"Help me! Someone, please, help!" My screams are frantic and bloodcurdling, but only last a breath of time before he jumps on top of me.

Pressure from his knee digging into my spine deflates my lungs. I try to scream for help again, but only a strained hiss is all that sounds.

"You fucking bitch!"

"Caleb stop!" I manage to wheeze.

My nails claw into the carpet in an attempt to escape because I'm scared to death of what he's going to do to me if someone doesn't stop him. The moment I gain a little traction and am able to move, I realize he's no longer on top of me and that we aren't alone.

The dark room grows loud with so much commotion that I can't even focus on what's happening as I shuffle back on my hands and feet. When my back meets the wall, I see silhouettes and find that Brody has Caleb restrained in a hold against his chest. Out of the corner of my eye, I catch movement and turn in time to watch Micah charge toward Caleb and barrel his fist into his face with a raging, "You motherfucker!"

An elixir of fear and anxiety detonates through my veins. Flames singe my throat when a deafening sob rips through me. I want to run for my life, but I'm trapped inside a paralyzed body. Another person barges into the room, followed by someone else. It's utter chaos, and I don't even realize Trent kneeling in front of me.

He takes my face in his hands, and with panic-stricken wide eyes, he urges, "Come on, Kate."

Trent grabs me from around my waist and pulls me onto my feet as Brody and a couple of other people fight Caleb to the ground. There's so much shouting and hysteria that I can't even hear my own crying. Someone shouts, "Get her out of here!" but Trent is already rushing me from the room.

Tucked under his arm, I keep my head down as he leads me through the party, blocking me as best as he can from the curious stares. It isn't enough, and it's as if I can literally feel their eyes all over me, touching me, judging me.

I'm mortified.

My darkest secret is out for everyone to see, and I lay waste to any self-worth I thought I had as tears free fall down my cheeks.

"Come on," Trent presses, leading me down the sidewalk.

He has me in his SUV so fast that I barely have my seatbelt on before he peels away. I can't bring myself to look at him. I don't know where we're going, but he eventually says, "You're coming to my place."

His voice is fierce.

"I want to go home," I mumble through my tears as I keep my focus on the streetlights passing by.

"Fuck that," he nearly shouts. "That dickfuck knows where you live. I'm not taking you home."

And he's right. Not only does Caleb know where I live but he also has a key. My hands tremble as I think about what he would do to me if he showed up in the middle of the night. If he got this out of control because I saw Trent at the beach, I can't fathom how he's going to react after watching me leave with Trent. The thought of it has me doubling over and resting my forehead on my knees as more tears come.

Trent places his hand on my back with a heavy, "You're going to be okay."

But nothing is okay. Everything is all wrong.

After he pulls in to the garage and parks, he helps me out and leads me inside and onto the elevator. He keeps me tucked under his arm, and I can't muster even an ounce of courage to say anything when we walk in his place and he takes me to his room, shutting the door behind us. He grabs a T-shirt and a pair of pajama pants from his dresser before taking my hand and leading me into his bathroom. He sets the clothes on the counter, and I keep my chin tucked down as he turns on the faucet.

"Come here," he says softly, reaching for my hand and pulling me over to him.

When he turns my palm up, I see the blood. In all the commotion, I didn't even realize how bad they had been cut. He puts my hand under the running water and carefully washes the dried blood from my forearm before doing the same with the other.

"Stay right here. I think Micah has a first aid kit in his bathroom." He rushes out, but he isn't gone for more than a minute before he returns with a bunch of bandages and a stack of washcloths. They land with soft thuds on the counter a second before he takes my hand back into his and examines the cuts for glass. "Does it hurt?"

I nod, too embarrassed to speak.

He handles me with care, meticulous as he scans each abrasion before applying ointment and bandaging me up.

It's humiliating.

He lifts my chin, but I don't dare look at him.

"Kate, please."

I shake my head, silently pleading with him not to make me talk.

"Please just look at me."

But I can't.

"This is killing me. I had no idea it was this bad," he says painfully. "This is fucking unimaginable. We need to call the cops."

"No!" I blurt. My heart rate spikes at the thought of going to the police. "My dad is a cop; he would find out." I drop my head again with a harrowing, "I can't."

"He can't get away with this."

"I just can't," I weep.

Fresh tears seep out and coat my cheeks, as his lips press against the top of my head and he whispers a heartbreakingly defeated, "Okay," into my hair.

A part of me wants to cling to him, bury my head against his chest, and beg him to fix this, to make it all go away. But I'm frozen, too scared to give into that want for fear of completely shattering under the weight of it.

After a moment, he slowly pulls away from me and soaks the washcloth under the warm water again. I wince when he presses the cloth to my cheek. He's being so gentle, but even that tiny pressure on my broken skin has fire skittering along my nerves.

"I'm sorry."

I stand still for him, but my mind is maniacal as it replays what just happened over and over again. Thoughts and visions overwhelm, and the walls begin closing in on me.

I step away from his touch with a meager, "I can do it."

"Kate . . ."

"Just give it to me," I say as I take the washcloth out of his hand.

Looking down at my feet, I wait for him to walk away from me, but he doesn't—not yet. "I'll go make an icepack."

I nod, and he goes, closing the door behind him.

I'm unmoving, my eyes still stuck on the floor, staring at my shoes that I put on a couple of hours ago.

A couple of hours.

Everything was fine. Today was fine. I was fine.

And now . . . now nothing is fine. In a slip of a moment, everything has changed.

Lifting my foot, I step over to the sink, toss the cloth aside and raise my eyes to the mirror.

I gasp when I see my reflection. It's haunting, but I can't look away because this has to be a mistake. This has to be some sort of a bad dream because the tragedy on the other side of the glass can't possibly be me.

She just can't be.

My face is splotchy from all the crying, my cheeks and jaw are already bruised, and my eye is nearly swollen shut. I can't look for too long before the reflection blurs into a muddling of watercolors as I begin to cry again.

Bracing my hands along the edge of the sink, I hang my head beneath a mountain of shame.

How could I have let this happen?

How does someone do this to a person they claim they love?

I was an idiot to have ever believed Caleb cared about me.

I never want to see him again.

The skin around my face grows tighter as it continues to swell, and I can't even stomach looking at myself. I'm beyond devastated. After all the times I defended him, my god, I can't even fathom what everyone must think of me.

I startle when the door opens and Trent steps inside with an ice pack for me. There isn't a hole deep enough for me to crawl into to hide from the humiliation.

"Can I help?"

I can't even give him a response as I stand here—a cowardly disaster.

"Will you let me?"

With hardly any strength left, I nod. What else do I have to lose? He couldn't possibly think any less of me at this point.

He takes the hem of my shirt in his hands, and I lift my arms as he pulls it off.

"Jesus," he breathes in, what I can only imagine is, disgust.

All it takes is one look at the bruises—both fresh and fading—that mark my shoulders and stomach for him to realize the ugly and shameful truth—that I'm a stupid girl who was dumb enough to allow my boyfriend to beat the shit out of me, while trying to convince everyone around me that he is a good guy. Completely resigned, I don't even bother trying to cover my body as he looks at everything Caleb's been doing to me.

With my eyes cast down, a tear slips along my lashes and drops to the floor. I can't do it—I can't be a part of his ridiculing eye as he stares at me. Covering my face with my hands, I crack, allowing a weak sob to break free. His arms come around me, and the touch is so profound that I lose all composure and crumple into him. Anguish wracks my body, and he only holds me tighter.

I wish to God that Trent didn't have to know this about me, but he does, and there isn't anything I can do to change that. It makes me feel inhuman in a way I can't really describe— gross, weak, ignorant, everything you would never want to feel. It crashes over me, burying me under its scrutiny, and I'm suffocating.

I step back, and Trent's arms fall away.

Holding out my hand, I ask, "Can you hand me the shirt?"

He does, and I pull it on before he gives me the pajama pants. As soon as I'm dressed, I walk into his room and slip into the bed. From my peripheral, I watch Trent change out of his clothes and into a pair of gym shorts before he slides in next to me.

He slips his arms around my battered body and pulls my head on to his chest. Tears steadily fall and land on his chest, which is now damp against my face.

"You're going to be okay." He keeps telling me this, but we both know it's a lie.

How could I possibly be okay after tonight?

How am I ever supposed to erase this from my memory?

Eventually, the tears run dry, leaving me numb and tired. In the warmth of Trent's bed, I somehow manage to fall asleep, but it's superficial. As I toss and turn throughout the night, my heart grows heavier and heavier with each passing second, minute, hour. Trent's arms have long since slackened around me, and I slowly push away from his body so I can look at his face.

Even in his sleep, his brows remain tense with concern or anger. He's going to have questions for me in the morning. Questions I don't want to face. Questions I won't have the answers to. He's going to want to know why.

But I don't know why.

All I do know is that I can't have him looking at me with judgment or pity or disappointment—the look that screams *I told you so.*

Quietly, I slip out of the bed and into the bathroom so I can change back into my own clothes. With my shoes in my hand, I cautiously pad over to his door and sneak out. When I peer down the hall, I see Micah's door is open, so I ease my way through the living room where I find my cellphone sitting on one of the end tables. I don't know who thought to grab it for me, but I'm thankful they did.

Once I manage to get out of the condo without waking anyone up, everything else happens in a series of motions that hold nothing more than a fog of gloom as I get onto the elevator and call for a cab to meet me downstairs.

When the taxi shows up, I open the door to get in and my phone rings. Trent's name flashes across the screen.

"Where to, ma'am?"

I silence the call and give the driver my address. I know I shouldn't go back there, but I figure I'll latch the swing guard so if Caleb tries coming over, he won't be able to get in.

My phone rings again. It's Trent.

Decline.
A moment later, it chimes with a text.

Trent: Where did you go?

The driver looks at me through the reflection of the rear-view mirror with curiosity. Who could blame him? He's got a girl in the back of his cab with a beaten face at three in the morning and a phone that's blowing up.

When it rings again, I decline it and then switch it over to silent.

Trent: Where the hell are you? Why did you leave?

Even when the cab pulls in front of the high-rise, my phone continues to buzz in rapid succession while I swipe my credit card and sign the receipt.

"Take care of yourself," the man says as I get out of the car.

I stand for a moment and watch as he drives into the night before I make my way inside and up to my floor, all the while my cell vibrates in the palm of my hand. Once I'm safe inside my condo, I lock the knob and the deadbolt and then flip the swing guard over.

Another round of vibrations shakes my phone, and I turn it completely off. Everything goes silent aside from the throbbing of my head that echoes in my ears. I toss my phone onto the bed as I head into my bathroom to find some migraine pills and some ibuprofen.

When I flick on the light, I nearly jump out of my skin when there's a knock on the door. I run and grab my phone, quickly powering it back on in case I need it. Standing in the threshold of my room, I stare at the door. Another knock sends my heart rate into overdrive, and I pad across the room, careful not to make a sound because I have no clue who's on the other side. It can only be one of two people: Caleb or Trent.

When I reach the door, I hold my breath as I lean in, peer through the peep hole, and look out.

Note From The Author

Read the conclusion to the Secrets & Truths Duet in
The Truths We Told

National Domestic Violence Hotline

If you are worried about your relationship or have questions
about your partner's behaviors, contact an Advocate.

They are available 24/7/365.

It's free and it's anonymous.

Call 1-800-799-SAFE (7233)

or chat online at
www.thehotline.org

Explore other titles from

e.k. blair

www.ekblair.com/books

Follow

e.k. blair

Instagram:
www.instagram.com/ek.blair

Facebook:
www.facebook.com/EKBlairAuthor

Twitter:
twitter.com/EK_Blair_Author

Goodreads
www.goodreads.com/author/show/6905829.E_K_Blair

Bookbub:
www.bookbub.com/authors/e-k-blair

Acknowledgments

It's no question that this needs to start with my husband. I know, I know—sappy—but truthfully, this book would've never happened if it weren't for his unyielding support.

Shawn, wow, where did you come from and how on earth was I lucky enough to find you? I realize I'm a handful and that I drive you crazy—after all, I'm an artist, I was born with crazy in my blood.

You don't often get the credit you deserve, so let me take this opportunity to tell you how appreciative I am of your constant love, support, and yes, toleration. By the blessings that be, you have embraced me wholly. There was a time I thought I was going to give up writing, but then you sat me down one night after dinner and asked, "Babe, what's your passion?" My response was easy: Writing. When you responded by saying, "Then write," you completely unraveled all my hesitations.

It was two words, two words you probably don't remember, but two words I will never forget. Like a strike of a match, you lit a fire inside me. I couldn't grab my laptop fast enough. I locked myself away, and this duet is the reflection of those two simple words.

Thank you for allowing me the freedom to chase my passion and live my dream. You'll never understand the therapy writing provides me—I'm inhuman without it. I know that seems strange, but let's face it, I am strange. Seriously, though, I love you so much for always being selfless with me. Again, thank you!

Sally, my wonderful assistant, where would I be without you? You are my secret weapon. Your unconditional support means the world to me. We've been through a lot—ups and downs and all arounds—yet, here you are, unwaveringly loyal. You push me when I need to be pushed, comfort me when I'm getting too stressed, guide me when I'm straying off track. More than anything, you believe in me. You *really* believe in me, and that alone is the best gift I could ever ask out of an assistant and a friend. I love you dearly, my Sally-boo.

My editor, Ashley . . . man, oh man, this manuscript challenged me in a whole new way. You told me to trust you when I wanted to run away. You knew this would be tough on me, and it was—it was very tough. But I trusted you, just as you had asked, and I am so glad I did. You're a tough editor, which is why I love working with you so much. You said to me, "I know this is going to be a lot of work, but I want you to be proud in the end." You were right. I put in the work that needed to be done, and I'm glad I did. I'm proud, thanks in large part to you!

I also what to acknowledge my PR team from Give Me Books Promotions for helping me launch this release, Champagne Book Designs for formatting, and to my readers— you guys are the icing on top of the cake for me, and I couldn't do what I do without you!

CPSIA information can be obtained
at www.ICGtesting.com
Printed in the USA
LVHW091316170320
650304LV00001B/104